W9-BAK-332

MY FATHER'S DAY GIFT

DAVID ANDREWS

Copyright 2014 David Andrews
All rights reserved.

No part of this book may be reproduced in any form or by electronic means, including information storage and retrieval systems, without written permission from the publisher, except by a reviewer, who may quote passages in a review.

Cover Design: Tracy Copes
Interior & Illustrations: J. L. Herchenroeder
Author Photo: JHU Public Affairs Office

Published by Bancroft Press
"Books that Enlighten"
P.O. Box 65360, Baltimore, MD 21209
410-764-1967 (fax)
www.bancroftpress.com

ISBN 978-1-61088-116-6 (cloth)
Printed in the United States of America

TABLE OF CONTENTS

To Pop

Preface

A Legacy of Inspiration

The cell phone vibrated in my pocket on June 22, 2011. A sneak peek at the screen revealed it was my mother. The dean of medicine at Johns Hopkins University was sitting next to me, adamantly appealing a contentious budget decision to our university leadership team. I decided that disrupting his argument by taking a call from my mother would be unprofessional.

Ten minutes later, during a break, I was able to return her call. The news was staggering. My 81-year-old father had just been diagnosed with pancreatic cancer. I'm not a physician, but I knew enough to realize that as lethal as many forms of cancer can be, only a few carry the implied death sentence of pancreatic cancer. That evening, I began writing this story.

Pondering life without my dad, I couldn't stop reflecting on his extraordinary impact. Episodes of great times and remarkable influence ran continuously through my mind. I wanted him to know exactly how much he meant to me. My dad was a proud but humble man of relatively few words. Long conversations about the meaning of our relationship weren't remotely in the cards. Nonetheless, I needed to demonstrate the depth of his meaning in my life. The story that follows became my vehicle.

As I wrote, I couldn't avoid thinking about other mentors who had shaped my life—relatives, friends, teachers, and coaches. I realized that I had the incredibly good fortune of growing up with the guidance of extraordinary male mentors. My father was the most influential, but just one of many. It dawned on me that I was truly blessed by this far-ranging support, and that all of these "fatherly influences" needed to be acknowledged.

Fiction, grounded in very real and meaningful experiences, evolved as the safest and most comfortable genre for me to convey my feelings. I've been told it's called a fictionalized memoir. All I know is that fictionalizing the events took pressure off of my memory and provides me a plausible defense to those who might remember the events differently. I also discovered that I could blend characters and events, reducing the risk of leaving an important mentor out of the story.

As my dad fought cancer, I continued to write and think more deeply about the way our lives are influenced by those who care for us. As a professor in education and child development, I've spent my entire career trying to understand and enhance the role of adults—parents, teachers, coaches, and mentors—in the lives of children. Faced with the mortality of my primary mentor, I began to see the issues more clearly.

Two simple and distinct messages came into focus:

Every interaction matters. In trying to explain and celebrate impact, we sometimes get caught up in the cumulative effect of a single individual. In truth, it's more about what is modeled during the most teachable and memorable moments than it is the collective influence of any one person. Highly salient events can happen at any moment and forever shape our future choices. My life's treasure is an extraordinary collection of memorable day-to-day interactions with my father and the other great men who are characters in this story.

Mentors are inherently memorialized. Early in the process, I was obsessed with letting my father know, albeit a bit indirectly, how much he had influenced my life. The obsession quickly extended to other mentors who crept into the story. I looked up old relatives, coaches, teachers, and neighbors, and sent them letters and drafts of "their chapters," generally trying to expunge the guilt of never having told them how much of a role they had played in my life. It took a while to realize that telling them, while appropriate and nice, was not the ultimate acknowledgement. We memorialize our mentors through deeply ingrained imitation. Role models become mentors when we replicate their actions. Living one's life consistent with what they've modeled for us is the ultimate acknowledgement of their influence.

More each day, I try not to take my good fortune for granted, for the truth is that too many young people don't have engaged fathers or caring mentors, and suffer substantially because of it. I hope this story connects with the mentor-rich among us, and inspires readers to take action to assure that all children and youth have the day-to-day support of a caring father and fatherly influences.

Rather than rely exclusively on the subtle messages of my own fictionalized memoir, I've added two sections at the end of this book in support of fathering and mentoring. The first section is the "Top Ten Ways to Honor Mentors." The second is a list of resources on getting optimally involved in the lives of young people.

I handed my dad a completed draft of *My Father's Day Gift* on the afternoon of June 16, 2013, the last Father's Day we would share. He was re-admitted into the hospital that evening and would never be discharged.

My mother read it to him as he struggled through his last five weeks of life. I held his hand as he passed away on July 21, vowing to lead a life he had modeled.

CREATIVITY

CHAPTER ONE

I rise at my usual time (just shy of 4 a.m.) and do my usual, slow, full stretch. Hands raised toward the ceiling, I slightly arch my back and lift up onto my toes. My muscles are only slightly limbered by this routine, so I ease carefully down the stairs, placing both of my hands on the parallel rails to allow my old knees time to reluctantly adjust to the weight-bearing demands of a new day.

The two dogs, waiting patiently at the base of the stairs, are well accustomed to my creaky descent at this early hour and synchronously ease into their own versions of the downward and upward dog stretches favored by yoga enthusiasts. The dogs' leisurely stretching and uninspired demeanor suggest they have no particular agenda for the day—until I unlatch the back patio door and slide the glass wide open.

They instantaneously launch into a mad dash, converting from lazy hounds to crazed canines. It's the same escape every pre-dawn morning, silently chasing something too dark for me to see—a critter, I suppose. Deer, rabbits, squirrels, raccoons, and opossum are all abundant on our 20-acre horse farm, and I regularly see the dogs chasing non-nocturnal critters during the day. I assume the game plan's the same in the dark, early-morning hours.

Suddenly, a black blur streaks between one of my pajama-clad legs and the partly opened back door. Before I can react, a stench attacks my nostrils, and my stomach immediately sours. My "just a game" theory about the morning dash is instantly dispelled. The dogs were indeed after formidable prey—a skunk!

I quickly slide the door shut to block out the next stinking streak. The closed door keeps the next odor-transporter out, but it also locks in a smell so noxious that I pull the bottom of my t-shirt up to my nose to keep from gagging. The entire house smells of putrid skunk. The source of the smell—our dog Bo—is no longer in sight. There's little doubt he's trying to hide from me, his own smell, or both.

I turn in circles until I discover that I'm getting repeated whiffs of my own pajamas. I can't follow the scent to track down Bo because it's all around me. The single moment Bo rubbed past my pajama leg was enough to permeate the fabric and ensure a request to Santa for a new pair come Christmas.

Bo is a two-year-old pit bull rescue pup, purposely mislabeled a "boxer-lab mix" to facilitate adoption, and a timid soul who tries his very best to follow the rules. On the rare occasions when he's caught in a misdeed, he's consumed with guilt and contrition. You can see it in his ears, his posture, and most strikingly in his eyes. He's the "King of Cower." If he thinks he's in serious trouble, he immediately heads to the confines of the sofa and curls into his penance-requesting position.

"The new beige sofa!" I shout, realizing where I'll find Bo.

Unconvinced the smell could get any worse, I turn the

corner toward the family room. The stench freezes me at the entrance. Scrunched deep into the corner of the just-purchased sofa is a shivering black ball of fur, dark eyes darting in panic, looking for some form of olfactory relief. Realizing that he can smell a stale potato chip on the floor thirty feet away, I can't imagine what's going on inside Bo's sensitive nose. My first reaction is to scream at the top of my lungs, "Get off the new sofa," but the immobilizing fear in his eyes fully registers just before I shout.

"Come on, Bo," I urge him quietly and kindly, hoping he'll slink toward me and the door without brushing against anything in his path. The gentle coaxing is in vain. Every step I take in his direction intensifies the aroma *and* the size of his round, black eyes.

As I approach, the t-shirt hem over my mouth and nose can no longer filter out the smell. I reflexively gag into the shirt. Fortunately, my stomach is empty and the heaves are mostly dry. I force myself to swallow a mouthful of acidic bile, figuring there'll be enough cleaning to do without spitting up on the carpet. The acid burns my throat, making me wonder what it does in my stomach. Are ulcers a foregone conclusion?

Fortunately, Bo is wearing his green paisley collar. I grasp it lightly, gently convince him to uncurl, and lead him off the sofa. A quick look and I'm briefly relieved it's no worse for the wear. Silly me. The damage to the sofa will leave no visual clue—purely an odious one.

Stooped and more firmly gripping his collar, I drag Bo

forward. He takes a few unwilling steps across the carpet, then locks his legs and slides several feet as we cross over onto the hardwood floor. He finally relents and reluctantly shuffles his four paws forward. He knows we're headed to the door, and I suspect he fears that the odor-spewing demon is still outside.

Approaching the sliding patio door, I anticipate another problem. Lola, the Weimaraner who's usually first to return from the morning romp, is pressing her nose against the glass, peering inside at the action. It doesn't take incredible foresight to understand that one of two things will be the case: she has the same contaminated scent or, as soon as the door slides open a crack, she'll dash inside, rub past Bo, and acquire it, compelling me to scrub it from her gray coat. I've yet to determine how to get the scent off one dog and desperately wish to avoid any more canines needing to be deodorized.

I ease the door open just enough to shoo Lola away with a quick thrust of my slipper. It's not necessary. As soon as the door cracks open, she recoils in horror and bolts back into the darkness. It takes a moment to realize that the smell escaping from the house is now stronger than the odor outside.

With Lola out of the way, dragging Bo out onto the patio becomes a cinch. I quickly step back inside, close the door behind me, and watch as he shivers on the door mat, barely avoiding the spotlight illuminating the front half of our red-brick patio.

Lola and Bo are now outside inhaling the fresh morning

air while I'm inside gagging. I wonder how far the scent has travelled in the house. Not only am I relieved that my wife Betty is away this Father's Day Sunday, but that I'll have time to get things back in some type of order before she returns tomorrow morning. How hard could it be? I'm not a Mr. Clean, but I've done my share of housework.

I decide to address the clean-up analytically and strategically, as any respectable university professor would, deducing that there are three places where the scent was most likely deposited: my left hand when it grabbed Bo's collar, my blue-striped pajamas, and the sofa. The pajamas and sofa can be easily removed from the house. The hand will take more effort. I decide to remove the sofa first, then the pajamas. This will allow me to handle everything that's been tainted prior to attempting to scrub the lingering scent off of my hands.

The easiest route to remove the sofa is out the front door. The double mahogany doors open wide. I momentarily worry about Bo rushing back in, but by now he's afraid of his shadow and I'm confident he's still sitting, shaking and petrified, on the edge of the back patio. Lola has already shown that she won't come near any entrance where the odor could seep out.

The sofa drags as easily across the hardwood floor as Bo and is on the front porch in minutes. I'm thankful it's an inexpensive sofa and not a pricey, heavy, fold-out sleep-couch. The image of the soiled sofa sitting on the front porch reminds me of college fraternity days when we strategically positioned a battered brown corduroy sofa on our apartment's front porch, allowing us both a comfortable beer-drinking and coed-watching position.

It's not yet daylight, so I decide to take my pajama bottoms off and leave them outside next to the sofa. The closest neighbor is nearly a mile away, so witnesses are unlikely. Returning inside, I stand pantless at the sink, furiously scrubbing my hands with soap. A quick sniff confirms that the flowery-smelling hand soap is no aromatic cure.

Didn't I read somewhere that juice removes skunk scent? Fruit juice? Apple? Orange? No, tomato juice! I approach the fridge, making certain to open the door with my non-scented right hand. There's apple, orange, and even strawberry-banana. No tomato.

I remember my Aunt Jane saying, with absolute certainty, that rubbing a handful of salt on your hands will remove your stinkiest smell. I open the pantry, again making sure to touch nothing with my contaminated hand. The big blue salt tube is close enough for me to grab with my clean hand. I pour a handful of salt into my cupped fingers, put down the tube, and begin rubbing my hands together. Repeating this exercise three more times, I'm hopeful that the smell has diminished. Another quick sniff of my left hand confirms that I'm wrong.

In desperation, I hit the liquor cabinet, searching for Bloody Mary mix. There it is—a full bottle of Mr. & Mrs. T. I'm tempted to get out the vodka as well, but am limited by having only one odor-free hand. I glance at the clock and vaguely remember once downing a vodka at 4:12 a.m. in my younger days. However, that was before going to bed, not after rising.

I set the Bloody Mary bottle on the counter, twist off the top, then pick it up with the same hand to pour out a generous amount. I scrub, repeat, and repeat again. This time, the sniff test is not too bad. Not odor free, but tolerable. The odor in the house lingers, even though I'm pretty sure that nothing else inside has been contaminated. Only one problem: While there may be enough Bloody Mary mix left in the bottle for a calming drink later, there's certainly not enough to clean Bo.

The iPad on the kitchen table should provide alternate remedies for deodorizing Bo. The sofa can wait. I sniff my hand before touching the delicate screen. How would you remove skunk juice from such a technologically sensitive surface? I wonder. I'm not sure how to remove fingerprints from the tablet, so I'd have no chance with skunk juice. I sniff the middle of my hand, then each digit, and determine that the smell on my fingertips is even fainter than the slight odor on the palm of my hand. Regardless, I Google "removing skunk odor" with the pointer finger of my odorless right hand.

The first site returned is that of a blogger who notes that vinegar and hydrogen peroxide are appropriate cleansers for skunk oil. Who blogs about cleaning? And who in hell blogs about cleaning skunk juice? In my current emergency, I only briefly question the blogger's credentials, and assume that all such bloggers are wise and practical.

I check the pantry, but there's only about half an inch of a $24 bottle of fine balsamic vinegar. It won't be nearly enough. Even if it were, it would leave the white spot on Bo's chest crimson. Likewise, I fear that the hydrogen peroxide would make his black coat match his white spot. I read on, and from the curiously detailed blog discover that an "over-the-counter douche" might do the trick.

My first thought: I never knew there was such a thing as a prescription douche. But there must be, given the blogger's need to make the distinction. Why, I wonder, would an over-the-counter douche be so much better at removing skunk oil than a controlled version?

It fascinates me for a moment how little I know about this feminine hygiene product. I've been married to the same woman for nearly thirty years and have never seen the inside of a douche box. I decide that this is a good thing.

Under Betty's counter in the bathroom? As I take quick and exaggerated strides up the stairs, I am physically reminded that I am still without pants. I detour into the bedroom and find yesterday's underwear and jeans crumpled on the floor next to the dresser, which may never again hold the pajama bottoms it stored the night before. I avoid the risk of contaminating the whole dresser. Instead of searching for new undies, I decide to re-wear yesterday's work clothes.

If Betty had been home, these clothes, used for mowing and weed-eating the day before, would already be washed, folded, and back in that same dresser drawer. The perspiration-and-grass-stained remnants of Saturday's chores certainly wouldn't be piled beside the same bed in which I'd slept. Yesterday's clothes, I decide, no longer contend for the worst-smelling items in the house, and I slip them back on.

I continue my douche search while again pondering how little I know about the product. Seems like I saw a box bearing the name somewhere in the house, but isn't it a bag? After all, kids jokingly calls each other "douche bags" when bantering, so a bag must be involved.

The douche box is exactly where I remembered seeing it, under the left-hand side of Betty's bathroom cabinet just beside the sink. The logo is so familiar. I've seen the ad for this product many times, but it was years ago and so subtle in guaranteeing "freshness" that I didn't know it was describing a douche.

"Douchebags," I mutter in reference to the marketing team that put the ad together, chuckling at my own lame joke.

I rip open the box expecting to find something exotic. It turns out that the bag is just a bag and calling someone a "douchebag" suddenly has very little meaning. It appears that the "bag" is not necessary unless you're going to use the douche in a very specific location. Bo's coat won't require such precision, and I decide to use a bucket instead.

I grab the shampoo from the shower and hustle back downstairs to retrieve a bucket from the laundry room, after which I head out onto the patio, where Bo still stands motionless in the dark. On a normal day, he runs from a bath, but today he's been paralyzed by his pre-dawn experience. After three application-and-rinse cycles with my wife's douche and another three with her shampoo, he remains scented, but in a much better and more familiar way. Fortunately, I'm not aroused.

As soon as I release him from the death grip that held him in place while bathing him, he heads into the darkness of the front pasture. I know from the tinkling sound of the tags on his collar that he's rolling his wet fur in the damp morning grass. I can only hope he hasn't decided that a fresh pile of horse manure is a better option than the douche.

It's not yet daylight, but I suddenly feel behind schedule—I've already lost precious time. The fear of procrastination that drove me from bed at four o'clock is back. It's already 5:20 and there's so much I want to do.

I dearly miss Betty when she's gone, but like most guys, I cherish the chance to experience certain freedoms rarely available during thirty years of marriage. Not freedoms that prompt me to stay out all night chasing young girls or drinking heavily, though a few beers and a cigar out by the pond aren't entirely out of the question. I'm much too old for such shenanigans, and I could never make my wake-up call should I attempt such things.

What I'm referring to is the freedom of a full day with no outside influence on my decisions. I can make my own choices and craft my own agenda, or have no agenda at all if I so please. That's the cherished gift of a fifty-five year old gentleman farmer left alone on his 20 acres. No "honey do" list today.

While I lack a formal list, there are dozens of things I've

been saving for this day. None would have made Betty's top ten priorities. Weeding flower beds, changing light bulbs, and washing the horses' water buckets are necessary and important tasks, but they can't compare with the things I have in mind.

Unlike her structured list, my list is a more random set of items that I've been wanting to accomplish "when I can find the time." I've never written them down or mentioned them to anyone. Some are big tasks. Others are very small. None is essential. Writing them down or communicating them in any way as an official list would redefine them as much less enjoyable.

In essence, they are "piddle."

When given full freedom, many men will piddle. That's what women call it when our priorities don't match theirs and the results are not as immediately obvious as they expect.

In my experience, the trick is to learn how to buy time, or earn "piddle points." It's sleight of hand learned only after years of marriage. I routinely scan the "honey do" list for things that appear to have grand, visible outcomes, but that take less time to accomplish than would be expected by someone who's never attempted the task and overestimates its complexity—typically one's wife. Completing these tasks with enthusiasm and pride early in the day, though not too quickly, deposits considerable piddle points into a guy's weekend ledger.

No need for such relationship games today. I've got all the piddle points I need and all day to piddle them away. It's my Father's Day gift to myself, but one whose mere acknowledgement would offend the loved ones unintentionally providing it with their absence. From my standpoint, their psyches will be best served if they spend the day feeling guilty that their busy lives left me all alone on such a big, important day.

One item on my morning agenda won't be altered, though—coffee! All of my adult life, I've made a fresh pot of coffee every morning before sunrise.

Monday, July 16, 1979

He was staring out the trailer window into the darkness when I awoke with my eyes burning from the tobacco smoke. We now refer to them as "mobile homes," but in the south in the late 1970s, political correctness wasn't necessarily extended to the white, working poor. It was still acceptable, at least where I grew up, to openly acknowledge that a loved-one lived in a trailer.

Inside the trailer was a round, Formica-topped table with a convenient panel on either side that folded up to yield more space in the cramped room. This morning, one side was down and was pushed flush against the bottom of the kitchen window.

The window looked out onto the tin-covered concrete slab that functioned as a front porch. Sitting at the end of the table angled toward the window, he searched the pre-dawn shadows.

I stopped in the trailer's kitchen doorway not eighteen

inches from the bedroom I'd just exited. He didn't change position, didn't alter his gaze, didn't even acknowledge my presence. The ashes on the cigarette he held loosely in his strong, stained fingers had grown long. Gravity bent the ashes toward the floor.

An empty coffee cup on the table was the only clue that, for him, this morning differed from any other morning of the past 53 years. Eight days prior, before my grandmother died, he would have been sitting in the same spot waiting for daylight, but his cup would have been full. Mildred, in her threadbare cotton gown, would have already made the coffee, while the slight, five-foot-seven-inch Gus would already have slipped into his blue Sears and Roebuck work pants and matching shirt.

At first, I thought the empty cup was symbolic of his loss. Perhaps sitting in front of the window with one of his favorite morning pleasures (the first cigarette of the day) but without the other (the first coffee) was his own, unknowing tribute to her memory.

"Uh-umm," I cleared my throat unnecessarily. Freed from his trance, but not startled, he looked in my direction.

Granddaddy Gus stood purposefully and made his way across the small kitchen to slowly open the cupboard directly above the empty coffee pot. He rifled through its contents, eventually securing filters in one hand and a tin can of Folger's coffee in the other. He stared at them like he'd discovered moon rocks misplaced by the Apollo 11 crew.

The empty cup, it turned out, had no symbolism at

all. Granddaddy Gus just didn't know how to make coffee. Over the next few days, I would learn that he couldn't make breakfast, do the laundry, buy groceries, or pay the bills, either. I watched him answer the phone, but I bet he didn't know which three-number combination to dial in case of an emergency.

Mildred and Gus were married at 15 and had my mother, Helen, at age 16. One might assume that hormones having kicked in, they had slipped away to share a night of teenage passion, and subsequently were forced to marry by strong Southern Baptist parents, worried about the family's image in their small, rural Georgia community. Not quite.

One spring day, my great grandmother left eight-year-old Mildred with distant relatives and never returned. While no one in our family has invested much time in genealogy, mention of my great grandfather is conspicuously absent and leads me to assume he might be unknown. I once heard that "he went to war." There's even a fuzzy, faded picture of a man in uniform, but I wonder. I assume that those who pursue the family's roots are looking for laudable links and traits. Those who don't bother to look sometimes fear that what they find will disappoint.

Gus's parents died when he was a young child, and he was raised, if you can call it that, by a bachelor uncle. Gus and Mildred met in the third grade. By all accounts, as sketchy as they might be, they instantly became the family neither ever had. By the ninth grade, they decided that marriage, not school, was their future. Mom was born a year later.

Never one to mince words, Mildred was graphic and excruciatingly direct. As an impressionable eight-year-old, I vividly remember her dispassionate description of her best friend's untimely death from a heart attack. "Mabel dropped dead!" she told my brother and me matter-of-factly.

Mildred dropped dead of a similar heart attack on July 6, 1979.

When we received the call, I was 20 years old and home from college, spending the summer doing odd jobs. She had always struggled with her weight, smoked like a chimney, and for years reported sporadic chest pains. Nonetheless, her sudden death shocked us all.

Over the next few days, the immediate family gathered in the small trailer. My mom, her sister and brother, their families, my father, and my brother all squeezed into the small space to comfort my grandfather. The funeral service attracted a few friends, but not as many as I expected. This was a woman who seemed to regularly draw unexpected visitors from the woods surrounding her secluded south Alabama trailer. The days after her death passed quickly and before the natural flowers accompanying Grandma Mildred from the funeral home to her grave site could fully wither, family members began excusing themselves back into their busy lives.

I wasn't due back at college until late August, and the odd jobs I was finding weren't generating much cash. My availability was noted by Mom and her siblings as they pondered ways to help Granddaddy through this difficult transition. I loved the crusty old guy and had always enjoyed spending time with him, so convincing me to change my summer plans was an easy sell. I happily agreed to stay on in the trailer and help Granddaddy build his new life.

As a psychology professor at a world-class university, I've had the good fortune to spend time with some pretty bright folks—noted scholars, university presidents, Nobel Prize winners, renowned business leaders, and even a few smart politicians who defied the apparent oxymoron. The next few weeks with Gus Payne, a man who initially couldn't make his own coffee, would confirm what I'd suspected for as long as I could remember: Granddaddy was one of the smartest, most creative people I'd ever encounter.

I'm not certain how much or how well he could read, but it didn't seem to matter. He had the uncanny ability to study objects and their function and recreate them regardless of their complexity. He would walk through Sears expressly looking for things he not only could make, but whose designs he could improve upon. He was a world-class engineer and inventor, a diesel mechanic trapped by poverty and a lack of educational opportunity.

When my grandmother decided to get into the ceramics business, Gus discovered a way to make molds that would reproduce any object she wanted for her inventory. She would purchase a ceramic vase at the discount store on Tuesday, he'd make a mold of it by Thursday, and by the weekend, they would be mass-producing as many copies of the trademark-violating object as time would allow. Unfortunately, the demand for these country-made ceramics was severely limited by my grandmother's taste for tacky vases, and by her lack of both patience and artistic ability in applying the finishing glaze. Gus made so many molds that he had to keep building additions to the shed he'd assembled for Mildred's business next to the trailer.

When he needed a new tractor, he pulled out his welder and started bending, cutting, and connecting metal until he'd designed and built a small tractor perfect for his needs—compact enough to make tight turns in a smaller garden, but with enough ground clearance to weed between the rows as the peppers, beans, and okra began to grow tall under the summer sun. A pea-sheller, an automatic watering device for rabbit cages, and a flat-bottom boat to navigate the shallows were among his innovations that left a mark on my childhood memory.

Most memorable, however, were the activities he crafted specifically for my brother and me. He once provided the materials and just enough guidance for us to discover the joy of nailing two ends of a long piece of old inner-tube to the trunks of two trees, creating a supersized slingshot capable of catapulting large, rotten watermelons toward the path travelled by younger, unsuspecting cousins.

When we were a bit older, he prompted us to discover fermentation, using scuppernong grapes, sugar, and a bit of yeast. Mom wasn't very happy when her young teens got tipsy tasting the results, but Granddaddy found it most entertaining.

His appreciation and commitment to "learning by doing" was ahead of its time, and he was a master at leading us to a solution without solving it for us. He once parked his old truck in the middle of a large field and asked if we wanted to drive it.

"Yes!" we screamed in delight.

"Keys are in it" is all he said.

We ran to the manual-shift truck, eager to take it for a spin around the open field. Obviously, we'd seen people drive, but we'd never paid much attention to manual shifting. Three days later, we were only able to move the truck a few yards before stalling the motor.

When we asked him to teach us to drive it, he answered with a question: "What do you need to know?"

Over time, we discovered that he only answered very specific questions, and even then, it would be with either a "yes" or a "no." We asked, "Does it have something to do with that stick in the floorboard?"

"Yes."

Then, "How about the pedals?"

"Yes."

"Will you show us?"

"No."

Through trial and error, combined with an occasional verbal affirmation, we finally discovered the basics, and after several days could jerk the old pickup around the field, much to Granddaddy's delight.

Of all our experiences with him, none had greater impact

than the frightening snake we encountered as pre-teens. Granddaddy hated snakes. If he saw a snake and could get his hands on a stick or a hoe, it was a dead snake. Poisonous or non-poisonous, it didn't matter. One day, as we were walking down from the garden to the trailer, a six-foot-long Sidewinder snake quickly slithered across the dirt road and into the grass on the other side. It looked particularly menacing because of its length.

Granddaddy sprang into action, searching for and finding a good-sized stick, then moving quickly to relocate the retreating snake in the grass. Impressionable and fearless when led by Granddaddy, brother Sam and I picked up smaller sticks and followed suit. Granddaddy brushed the grass back and forth with the stick until he found the back half of the snake. The front half was already half-way down a hole. Granddaddy took a couple of wild swings at the fast-moving tail, but the snake disappeared before Granddaddy could inflict any observable damage.

With the snake now safely in the hole, Granddaddy looked at us and asked, "Ideas?"

Sam immediately spoke up. "Smoke him out!"

I wasn't exactly certain where Sam got the idea or what he had in mind, but it sounded like fun to me. "Yeah!" I shouted.

Granddaddy slowly walked about twenty yards to the shelter he'd built for his homemade tractor. He retrieved a red, metal, two-gallon can of gasoline. We waited at the snake hole. When Granddaddy returned, he handed the can to Sam and his cigarette lighter to me. I immediately thought how fortunate we were that our mother wasn't around.

Sam smiled broadly and immediately began pouring gasoline through the spout into the hole. Granddaddy let him pour about half a gallon before putting his hand on Sam's shoulder as an indication that he'd used enough. I was moving in quickly with the lighter when he stopped me too with: "Whoa, there!"

Undoubtedly thinking twice about the wisdom of letting his eleven-year-old grandson throw fire into a hole just filled with gasoline, he took the lighter from me and motioned for me to move to the side of the hole. As a diesel mechanic, he always had handy a dirty rag to check whatever fluids were in question. He pulled the old rag from his back pocket, took my stick, wrapped the rag around the stick, poured a small amount of gasoline on the rag, and lit it.

Now holding my shoulder to make sure I stayed to the side of the hole, he handed me the unlit end of my four-foot stick. I immediately thrust the fire rag toward the hole. The moment the rag touched the saturated earth, flames were sucked deep inside. Seconds later, the ground beneath us rumbled as fire shot two feet into the air.

"Maaaannnn," Sam drawled, stretching out the word as only a Southern youngster could.

"Yeah, how ya like that, snake?" I added with pride, handing the stick to Granddaddy.

The fire on the stick and around the hole quickly extinguished itself, but Granddaddy stomped around the grass at the hole's edge to make certain.

"Show's over," he said, and we turned from the hole and headed toward the trailer.

With no warning, six feet of snake suddenly flew from the hole as if shot from a cannon, its head fully engulfed in fire. Sam and I never saw it fall dead to the ground. We were dashing to the trailer, not taking precious time to look back. When we reached the safer confines of the porch, we finally glanced back to see Granddaddy, bent over and slapping both thighs in laughter. The snake lay with smoking head in the grass by his side.

Those precious boyhood memories were challenged in the weeks after my grandmother's death. Yet, quickly I began to understand.

It wasn't that Granddaddy couldn't figure out how to make coffee. He'd simply never had reason to think about it. For 53 years, his coffee was waiting for him whenever he made his way to the kitchen table. He never thought much about how it got there. The division of responsibility in Gus and Mildred's life was complete. Making coffee was as foreign to Gus as changing the carburetor on a pickup truck would have been to Mildred.

That first morning, I feigned my own coffee-making ignorance to reduce his embarrassment, and when we made it together, we were silently proud of our success. This respectful approach defined our relationship for the next few weeks as together we "figured out" how the washing machine and other appliances worked, where the extra toilet paper was stored, and which brand of peanut butter was our favorite.

Making coffee was the first of many collaborative efforts to recreate the life Mildred had built and maintained for him. We cooked bacon in the cast iron skillet and floated fried eggs in the residual grease. We made grits, reading the required ratio of grits-to-water from the round container but eventually guessing about the amounts because Mildred's kitchen wasn't equipped with measuring devices.

On that very first day, Granddaddy decided he could help me develop a few new skills of my own. Semi-retired from his lifelong job as a diesel mechanic, he continued to use his mechanical skills to provide low-cost repairs to friends and neighbors with ailing farm equipment. As soon as he finished breakfast, he stood up and donned a bright yellow Caterpillar cap.

"You comin'?" he said, walking toward the trailer door.

He was on his way out to work and expected me to join him. I was still in shorts and a t-shirt. Dishes remained on the table and a skillet of warm bacon grease was still on the stove, surrounded by a carton of eggs and uncooked bacon.

By the time I threw on some jeans, stashed the remaining eggs and bacon in the refrigerator, collected the dirty dishes in the sink, and hastily used a few sheets of single-ply paper towel to rake off table crumbs, he was sitting in the truck. By the time I slapped some peanut butter onto bread slices for our lunch and filled the thermos with what was left in the coffee pot, the truck motor was running.

As we pulled away from the trailer, the sun peeked over the horizon. We followed the dirt road to a paved county road, then to the potato farm where we would spend the day. The potatoes were ready for harvesting, but the "tater digger" was broken. We spent the better part of the morning largely in silence, trying to figure out what was wrong with a conveyor belt designed to transport freshly dug potatoes off of the ground to a height allowing them to free-fall into a truck.

He stood patiently as I traced the intended path of the potatoes up the conveyor belt. From a distance, he watched as I pulled on this and that, started the engine to see what moved and what didn't, and eventually noticed that one rotating cog in the overall scheme of parts moved freely without engaging any others.

As soon as I made this discovery, he moved in and handed me the perfectly-sized wrench to remove the bolt that would allow us to replace the pin, which had sheared off when the belt became overloaded with potatoes. The replacement pin was in his pocket. Obviously, from the time of our arrival, he had understood the problem and solution just as well as I had understood how to make coffee.

While I felt a great sense of accomplishment in finding the problem on my own, no big celebration erupted in support of my discovery. We changed the pin and unceremoniously moved on to other farm-fixing tasks. By three o'clock, we finished our work and headed back to the 10-acre woods and the trailer.

Granddaddy entered and went straight back to the small bathroom to wash his grease- and grime-ridden hands. While presumably clean, there was little change in their appearance after washing. They always looked like he'd just closed the hood of a broken-down dozer.

I filled the kitchen sink with hot water to wash the breakfast dishes, lamenting the lack of an automatic dishwasher. He assumed his usual position at the kitchen table, gazing out the window.

It took me a short while to figure out that he was waiting for supper. Country folks, especially older country folks, eat early. It was 4:00 p.m., we had just walked in the door, and he was ready for supper.

Two weeks earlier, he would have entered the trailer to the smell of fried chicken and Crowder peas—not the little frozen green peas you get from a bag, but fresh brown Crowders resembling black-eyed peas, only much smaller. The peas would surround a ham hock in a bowl already placed on the table, along with piping-hot fried chicken and warm rolls. He would have followed the same path to the back of the trailer to wash his hands. On his way, he would have passed by Mildred, standing in front of the stove, and pinched her butt. She would have playfully called him a "bald-headed bastard." After his failed attempt to change the appearance of his hands, he would return to join her at the table, where his plate would be full and waiting. This three-minute ritual had defined the end of his every workday for over five decades.

Now there was no fried chicken, and there were no Crowder peas. He seemed puzzled that dinner hadn't found its way to the table.

I rummaged through the fridge looking for something I could make quickly. Fortunately, a turkey carcass was left over from our days of mourning.

I pulled meat from the carcass and began boiling water for rice. He sat staring out the window while we waited for the water to boil.

It's said that a "watched pot never boils." Neither of us was actually watching the pot, but his outward, silent gaze made it seem like hours before the first tiny bubble rose to the surface. We'd said very little to each other all day. He rarely spoke. As a child, I was usually verbose (I've remained so into adulthood), but I respected my grandfather's pithy communication and responded in his presence only when necessary. This current silence, however, was profoundly different from the working silences of learning by doing.

I'm not certain he'd ever thought about how dinner, like morning coffee, made its way onto the table, nor that he appreciated the challenge of having chicken, peas, and whatever else hot and on the table at the exact moment he walked in from a hard day's work.

We made it through the day and the weeks that followed without starving. After I went back to school, Gus didn't die of loneliness. Rather, he engaged his innovative mind in solving household challenges. The second week, he bought a microwave. Mildred never had a microwave, and Granddaddy Gus took great pride in discovering what he considered innovative technology perfectly suited to his needs. He was not threatened by his lack of knowledge because none of his peers, male or female, could use a microwave either. Through pure experimentation, he learned to microwave most of what he needed and took quiet but obvious pride in his new skills.

I left him, having gained a few new mechanical skills and a much deeper understanding of how necessary my grandparents were to one another. I also walked away from the smoky trailer with an insight into learning that would permanently shape my professional and personal life. Sometimes folks have to figure things out for themselves. They don't always need a lecture from a professor. They just need a little support and the right wrench, or microwave, or douche, at just the right time.

One of Gus's favorite sayings was, "If you're not going to use your head, you might as well have two asses." He used this phrase to characterize questionable choices I'd made as a child. I fully expected to hear it many more times during the weeks after my grandmother's passing. I didn't hear it that first day, or ever again.

RESTORATION

CHAPTER TWO

If it had been a normal Sunday, not to mention one that hadn't started with the skunk fiasco, I'd have drunk another cup or two of coffee, answered a few e-mails, checked on the Indians in the baseball box scores, and tried to avoid the usual reading and writing that can easily consume a professor's weekend.

Today, though, wasn't a normal day. It was my day to piddle—even waste if I wanted. With the skunk episode already taking a chunk out of my piddle day, I was anxious to get it back on track. The faintly discernible silhouettes of the fences and the barn signaled the early stages of daybreak. I relished these quiet early mornings on the farm. As horrifically as the day started, the emerging familiar shapes provided hope that the new light would unveil more fulfilling activities.

I squint to see the real reason we moved to the farm—Betty's beloved quarter horse, Eugene. The back patio provides the same vantage point as the kitchen window, and from this angle, even in this light, I should be able to see him sticking his head out of the stall window.

Where is that big boy? I wonder.

Betty and I grew up in suburban middle-class neighborhoods. Like many kids growing up in such surroundings, we travelled through beautiful horse-laden country on the way to visit distant relatives, and we both longed for a horse. I would cover my eyes when passing horses in their green pastures and whine, "If I can't have one, I don't want to see one."

Betty expressed her unmet desire by dedicating her annual birthday wish, the one that comes with blowing out the candles, to owning a horse. She claims to have made no other wish since she was five years old. On her fiftieth birthday, her wish came true.

Despite our childhood longings and over twenty years of decision-making as a married couple, we had never seriously considered owning a horse. We managed to get sporadic equine fixes through occasional trail rides at typical tourist spots, with haggard horses for hire and an ever-chatty wrangler who, like a second grade teacher monitoring the walk to the lunchroom, chastises riders whose horses wander out of line.

During these trail rides, we never talked about exchanging our very comfortable suburban lives for a totally different one requiring the dedicated care of our own horses. However, when our oldest of two children left for college, Betty's once evenly-divided maternal attention suddenly shifted exclusively to the younger one who remained at home. In many ways, the "baby" enjoyed the extra attention, but from my perspective, it hinted at smothering. Given that the kids are two years apart, I began to do the math. In two years more, the next maternal attention switch would have

Betty's attention focused squarely on me.

I immediately began searching for a distraction. A friend with horses was constantly lamenting the time and attention they require. When she announced that one of her mares had just foaled the perfect birthday horse, we became horse people. I purchased the adorable foal with absolutely no knowledge of what it takes to care for a horse, deciding to rely completely on my belief that whatever care was necessary would be enough to keep Betty's attention.

I kept the foal's existence a secret from Betty for nearly two years—the time it takes before a colt is old enough to train and ride. The timing was perfect. Our youngest would be headed to college and the colt's "maturity" would coincide with my wife's 50th birthday, yielding the surprise present of a lifetime. (Those who know horses realize that maturity is not the apt way to describe a two-year-old colt, but that's another story.)

A surprise present not yet received, the horse became known to everyone except Betty. Our children, my in-laws, my parents, friends, and siblings all visited "the horse" during those two years, without her knowledge.

We even named the horse, knowing full well that this should be her prerogative. This at least was due to a promise we had made to the children when we left the west coast and moved to the mid-west; we had attempted to comfort them by suggesting that they name our next pet after our home town of Eugene, Oregon. It turned out the next pet was Betty's horse, and we began calling him Eugene. It stuck before Betty ever met him.

Forty-five cakes and 1,265 candles later, Betty's earliest birthday fantasy came true and Eugene changed our lives forever.

My understanding of equine financing proved as naïve as my knowledge of horse care. It turns out that purchasing the horse is unequivocally the cheapest aspect of ownership. Horses need stuff—lots of stuff. Horse owners need even more stuff.

When we became parents for the first time, I was amazed at the stuff that a new infant required. The stuff needed by an infant pales in comparison to the stuff required by a horse. Strollers, car seats, rattles, diaper bags, cribs, changing tables, high chairs, and other infant stuff adds up. Horse stuff adds up quicker. Saddles, saddle pads, bridles, halters, lead ropes, lunge lines, brushes (lots of brushes), hoof picks, blankets, feeders, fly masks, horse trailers, and on and on.

Furthermore, the stuff required by a horse is considerably bigger and more expensive than the stuff required by a new infant. Even with the rapidly escalating cost of fancy strollers, the comparison with purchasing a horse trailer is enough to make the point. The most expensive new stroller is considerably less than one-tenth the price of the lowest-cost horse trailer. Both are required to move often unwilling mammals farther than they can, or are willing to, travel under their own power.

For us, the expense was multiplied by the decision to have Eugene live with us. After 45 years of waiting, Betty was making up for lost time. We started looking for farms immediately. As we searched, previously undisclosed aspects of her equine fantasies began to be revealed.

As I found out, her simple childhood wish for a horse had secretly matured over the years into something more. She began to describe, in elaborate detail, the perfect home for Eugene. It was becoming clear that the horse's quality of life was about to dramatically improve. I was beginning to wonder about mine.

Betty could picture a long winding driveway with four-rail black fencing defining the lush pastures on each side, Eugene out front grazing when she came home from work. She further fantasized about him trotting beside the car as she headed down the drive toward the house. I suspect there were moments in the fantasy when Eugene was being ridden by a shirtless romance-book cover-model with long flowing hair. If so, she was discreet enough not to share.

She did, however, describe the barn, the pastures, the riding trails, and the sunset views from horseback—in fact, everything down to the Christmas wreath to be placed on Eugene's half-stall door, complete with apples and peppermint sticks within his easy reach. Ironically, the fantasy details became fuzzier when I probed about the condition of *our* abode—the place where *we* would stay while Eugene enjoyed the lifestyle of the rich and famous.

We could afford a farm and a comfortable lifestyle for both horses and humans. However, it was a financial reality that as the lifestyle of one mammal improved, that of we humans would suffer. Our search to find a farm presented a much clearer understanding of whose quality of life would be improving.

To Betty, the daily greeting ritual was as important as the location and orientation of Eugene's stall window. Betty could graphically describe waking in the morning and opening the kitchen blinds to see Eugene sticking his head out of his stall window. She would tiptoe across the dew-covered grass leading to his stall window and give him a morning apple in return for a nuzzle on the cheek. Again, exactly where and when I would get my nuzzle was ill-defined.

Realtors should be judged on their listening skills. Ours was listening carefully to Betty's dream. After a few disappointing showings of farms with great people-accommodations but marginal horse-digs, the realtor, careful not to oversell, indicated that she had a place she thought might be an option. It had been on the market for a while and the house would need "some work," but the description made it sound perfect for horses.

As we approached the farm and passed the for-sale sign near the entrance, you couldn't miss the beautiful bay horse grazing aimlessly in the weedless, lush front pasture. I was immediately suspicious, given that Eugene is also a dark brown bay with black mane and tail. We turned into the drive and the horse, as if on cue, began to trot alongside the fence. The fence was a dull gray, but I was already calculating what it would cost to paint it fantasy black.

We parked on a dusty gravel drive in front of the Tudor-style house, which from the outside looked dated but livable. Upon entry, I could sense Betty's fading enthusiasm. She was a giddy five-year-old during that horse escort up the drive, but was coming to grips with where, as an adult, she might have to sleep and eat. The house was very clean but considerably outdated, with décor that can only be described, euphemistically, as eclectic—pink shag carpet; glue-on mirror tiles randomly stuck to drywall; dark, cheap paneling in some places and blonde, lightweight wooden beams in others; and light fixtures from multiple, unidentifiable eras.

I found it strange that the realtor said very little as we entered the foyer. She ushered us across the faux brick flooring, quickly moving toward the kitchen, which, with self-painted cabinetry and bright, fruit-themed wallpaper from the '70s, was clearly not the strongest sales feature. The rope lighting hastily tacked under the cabinets for ambiance did little to improve the disappointing effect of the orange-tinted laminate countertops.

The realtor, however, marched us straight toward the caramel-colored porcelain sink, which was chipped and faded. There was a window directly in front of the sink, and she quickly grabbed the cord to the dingy vinyl shades and pulled them wide open. The move was so dramatic that I wondered why she didn't simply twist the rod to position the vinyl slats so we could see through. Suddenly, the desired effect was all too clear.

Another bay gelding—this one with a white star on his forehead—was staring straight at us through a stall, the window providing the picture-perfect frame. Had we told the realtor that Eugene had a white star perfectly centered on his forehead? Without so much as a quick glance in Betty's direction, I realized we had just bought a farm.

I continue to peer out the kitchen window as the emerging daylight exposes the now famous stall window. Eugene's head isn't protruding as it does every morning in anticipation of the driving force in his life—no, not Betty, but food. He must be nosing around on the stall floor in search of a blade of hay that he somehow overlooked in the darkness of night. He will make a quick and vain search on occasion, but usually returns immediately to stare at the house, waiting for a sign that breakfast is on its way. I watch for a minute or two but see no movement.

Realizing that Bo and I had provided Eugene with ample entertainment with our skunk-cleaning show, I wonder why he isn't watching intently, a bit agitated that such a fiasco might delay his morning feed. He still shows no sign of being in the stall.

Suddenly fearing the worst, I bolt through the back door onto the patio, startling the finally relaxed hounds, and briskly move across the wet grass in my bare feet, eyes fixed on his stall window. *What if he has colic*—horse talk for stomach discomfort—*and has gone down?* My thoughts immediately shift to a task that would make skunk juice-cleaning a picnic—telling Betty about Eugene's demise.

Reaching the window, I grab the frame and pull myself up on my tiptoes to peer into the still dark shadows of the stall. My line of sight allows me to see the center of the stall floor. Eugene's bulky frame is not in view. The corners remain obstructed and I panic, thinking that he might have "cast"—horse talk for inadvertently wedging himself into a corner where he'd roll in discomfort.

Heart now racing, I move quickly toward the barn's large sliding front doors and pull hard to budge the rusty hardware upon which the heavy wood hangs. As I pry the doors open, "Spooky," the black barn cat, slips quickly past my leg. Usually elusive and totally unengaged, the cat stops abruptly and stares back curiously over his shoulder. I can't confirm it, but I believe he actually wrinkled his nose at my smell. Is it the skunk juice on my hands or the day-old undies?

As the rising sunlight illuminates the aisle between the stalls, the panic over Eugene's potential cast and colic is replaced by an entirely different anxiety. His stall door is wide open, so he definitely isn't lying inside. I immediately strike out on the path that I know will lead me to him.

I run through the aisle, past the four other horses in the small front barn, glancing at each stall door to be sure that Nellie, Lacy, Mojito, and Macho Man are all secure. As I rush by, Nellie, my paint horse, confirms her presence with a recognizable neigh. She, too, knows where I will find Eugene and is noticeably jealous.

Approaching the end of the short aisle, I see the second telltale sign that I'm heading in the right direction: a 12-foot-long, two-by-six board which usually runs parallel to the ground at shoulder level to the horses. The board secures the opening between the stall aisle and the indoor riding arena. This morning, it's across the opening but lies flat in the arena sand.

A similar board separates the opposite opening of the arena from the feed room beyond. I sprint through the length of the arena with bare, damp feet, collecting a thick layer of arena sand, and approach the cross board protecting the feed room. I don't need to look. I know that the other board will also be flat on the ground, having served as no barrier to Eugene's final destination. I step over the board and look to the right, where I know he'll be standing. Yep, his big horse's ass is facing me, his head buried in the galvanized metal garbage can that holds his beloved sweet grain.

Shouting "Eugene" has no noticeable impact on his single-minded mission. He continues to crunch loudly, ignoring me as I grab his mane and yank upward. I slap his big butt like a cowboy trying to start a stampede. Nothing will dislodge his huge lips from the surface of the grain that's now less than one-third of the way from the bottom of the container. When I finished feeding last night, the grain was well over two-thirds full. As I mentally calculate the volume of his consumption, I shudder.

Concern shifts to anger as I realize the situation he's created. Not only is he ruining my piddle day, he's harming himself. The only way I know to truly get his attention is with physical force. With no obvious alternative, I decide that a somewhat gentle knee to the rib cage might get him to lift his head. I rehearse saying the words "somewhat gentle" in preparation for the story I will later recount to Betty.

I'll never admit that it takes quite a bit of physical force to get his attention with this technique. Nor will I admit that I've been physical with him in the past. Sometimes, with horses at least, the ends justify the means. Yet, I continue to wonder if there isn't another way. Am I trying to get him out of the grain quickly, or am I now so angry at him that I'm quick to consider aggression?

Without further thought, I deliver a sharp knee directly to his rib cage. Eugene startles, moving his body to the side quickly and raising his head completely from the can—just the response I was seeking. If I were a well-heeled cowboy, I would have had the halter raised to head height and quickly slipped it over his head to lead him back to his stall. Like the greenhorn I am, I failed to grab his halter from outside his stall, or from any of the other stalls I passed on the way to the feed room. I try to wrap my left arm around his raised head, but he quickly sidesteps me, dips under my grasp, and returns to the bottom of the grain can.

Realizing that a couple more minutes of gorging won't change his prognosis, I run back across the arena, retrieve a halter and lead line, and hustle back to the feed room. My feet are now caked with arena sand as if I've just left the ocean surf and am heading back to my towel on the beach. I wish.

Horses are initially afraid of, and uncomfortable with, many things, but they get used to things very quickly, *habituate* in horse parlance. My second knee to Eugene's rib cage has no effect and I'm forced to consider a third. Getting angrier by the second, I decide that escalating force is not the sole solution. When I knee him even harder, he lifts his head. This time, I'm fully prepared with the halter.

The magical powers of a thin piece of nylon, placed strategically around a trained horse's head, always amazes me. With the halter in place, a 1200-pound beast that had to be physically and aggressively forced to raise his head from the grain and could effortlessly drag the world's strongest man through the thick arena sand calmly follows me back to the barn.

After he's safely in his stall, I immediately lean down to feel his front hooves. As expected, they're not hot to the touch but noticeably warm. The hooves of a healthy horse are cool. The hooves of a horse with laminitis are warm. If the laminitis is severe, the hooves are actually hot to the touch. Laminitis is one of a horse owner's greatest medical fears. It's caused by many things, but essentially by an overabundance of blood in the hooves. The painful result, commonly called foundering, can severely and permanently damage the structure and function of the bones in the hoof, rendering the horse permanently lame.

Laminitis can be caused by overeating—a carbohydrate overload. The rich, pooling blood in the nonporous hooves creates too much energy and leads to serious damage. The condition causes great discomfort. It's difficult to watch a horse struggle with this condition when it gets severe. Irreparable damage to the hooves leads many horses to be euthanized.

Memories of Kentucky Derby star Barbaro "foundering" after surgery, and being put down because of laminitis, run through my mind as I check each warm hoof. Like Eugene, Barbaro was a beloved Bay with a beautiful star on his forehead.

Bute and Banamine are the only two horse drugs I've ever heard of, and I know Eugene has had some of each. Horse people toss around the names of these two drugs like a chef refers to salt and pepper. Bute and Banamine are the ibuprofen and antacids of the equine world. Unfortunately, I can't remember which is described as horse Advil and which is described as horse Tums.

"Such a greenhorn!" I mutter.

Fortunately, the young vet who was last out to check the horses used a bold, black Sharpie to label each bottle. One's labeled "Pain and Swelling," the other "Cholic/Upset Stomach." My best diagnosis of Eugene is pain caused by an upset stomach. Uncertain what to do, I decide to give him a little of both drugs.

Each treatment is in a container that is a cross between a medical syringe and the tube used to re-caulk bathroom tile. Theoretically, one inserts the tip of the tube into the very back corner of the horse's lips and squeezes a portion of the gooey substance directly into the horse's mouth.

Having tried this a few times, I have to presume that horses cannot spit. It's obvious they don't like the procedure and make an effort to push the medication out of their mouths by repeatedly and forcefully moving their tongues forward against the top of their mouths, but they never spit. I've actually been spat upon by a billy goat, and understand from friends who've visited Peru that llamas are impressive spitters. Horses obviously aren't.

A skilled veterinarian can swiftly administer medication deep enough into the back of the mouth that the horse will make a few tongue motions but swallow completely before losing any of the medicine. With me, it takes a few tries to position the container of Bute in the corner of the mouth and, by the time I squeeze, Eugene has moved his head. The tip of the container is barely in the side of his mouth. I squeeze anyway. Some goes into his mouth while a substantial portion drops to the stall floor. Even more of the medication falls to the floor as Eugene pushes his tongue forward repeatedly, leaving me to wonder if he benefitted at all from the attempt. Nonetheless, I move on to the Banamine, but the process is about as unsuccessful.

Betty loves Eugene, but he's not an exceptionally talented horse. He knows the basics. He can whoa, go, change speeds, turn at the request of even novice riders, and stand for grooming. He has no real bad habits, and that's about it. On the other hand, he has neither the breeding nor training to win anything other than an occasional "Participant" ribbon at a beginning-level youth show—that is, if Betty would ever require him to take part in such a strenuous display of walking and trotting.

Nonetheless, Eugene has one extraordinary skill. He is the consummate escape artist—the Houdini of equines. Eugene escapes his stall using a series of sophisticated maneuvers that begin with him reaching over the Dutch door and lifting the metal latch with his lips, which he holds together long enough to slide the latching apparatus two full inches to the right. (With such mouth-related dexterity, why can't he spit?)

No other horse in the barn shows any interest in the latch. I assume this is because they have no concept of the relationship between the cold metal structure and their imprisonment in the stall. After removing the latch, Eugene simply walks forward, pushing the door open with his chest, and proceeds directly to the opening of the indoor arena. At the 12-foot opening, he grabs the 2" x 6" x 10' cross-board with his teeth and lifts it up from its holder. He then lowers the board to the arena floor and gently steps over it, careful not to trip. Then he moves quietly, yet excitedly, across the arena toward the feed room.

When confronted with another cross-board, he repeats the action that removed the first. This one, however, is a secondary precaution placed directly against a large sliding metal door that further protects his prize. No problem. After removing the cross-board, he sticks his nose directly into the corner where the heavy, closed sliding door meets the side of the barn, pushes hard with the tip of his nose, and wedges one of his front hooves into the corner for additional leverage. The simultaneous pressure of his nose and hoof are enough to move the door a few inches and create a gap large enough to accommodate his full snout. From this position, he simply walks forward using his enormous mass to force the sliding door open.

Once inside the grain room, Eugene moves directly to the feed can. The lid is always firmly in place on the galvanized metal trash can. However, the handle was designed for a human hand to grasp easily and pull up. If unlatching the stall and removing the cross-boards are easy for Eugene, this is the simplest task of all. He grabs the handle with his teeth and, in one swift motion, flings the lid across the room. Now, it's simply eat until the food's gone, or until you get caught.

Eugene can unlatch his stall in about 15 seconds and can be standing at the grain bin, his head buried in it, 90 unsupervised seconds later. You can observe and document the entire process, but only if you hide. Like a convicted felon, Eugene knows not to attempt escape when anyone is watching.

We've learned to keep a second clip on his stall, one that we trust requires more dexterity to unlatch than is present in a horse with a big thick tongue and flappy lips who can't spit. This morning, the second latch is lying on the floor at the opening to the stall. I either failed to clip it last night, or Eugene has been working after hours on his dexterity.

Guilt, anger, and fear simultaneously consume me as I stand next to Eugene in the wash rack, hosing cold water onto his hooves. The vet prescribed cold running water the last time Eugene managed a grain-gorging escape. The water will help cool his warm, inflamed hooves and relieve some of the discomfort.

I patiently move the tip of the hose from one hoof to the

next, rubbing his shoulder and neck as he stands motionless. The water must feel good on his hooves. He sighs, flapping his big lips appreciatively. Nonetheless, I'm so angry that it's difficult to sympathize with his self-inflicted plight and I have to force myself to continue the cold water treatment.

I know Eugene is not feeling well because he doesn't flinch when my cell phone rings in my pocket. Under normal conditions, unexpected noise would startle him. The phone is deep in the front pocket of my tight jeans and impossible to fish out while managing the hose. Even if it were easy to retrieve, now's not the best time to be taking a call. I let it ring into voicemail, briefly forgetting it's Father's Day.

I tend to Eugene for another hour, running cold water on his hooves, leading him on short walks in the arena, and constantly monitoring his well-being, suspecting he'll lie down and colic. Despite my disappointment in how this will change my day, and despite my anger over his choices, his sad helpless eyes keep eliciting an otherwise unexplainable compassion, making it difficult for me to leave his side.

Tuesday, October 22, 1974

Monday morning homeroom was nearing an end when Coach Price tried desperately to check the roll. Thirty uninspired high school seniors milled about, largely ignoring the seating chart designed to facilitate the morning attendance review. The new teacher, doubling as a first-year football coach, had given up trying to get us into our assigned seats after the first two months of his young teaching career.

He refused to tell us his age, but his inexperience was obvious to even the most unobservant student. We speculated that he had been in our seats only four to five years prior.

His wavy brown hair hung considerably farther over his ears and collar than the hair of his older colleagues, and his eyebrows were barely visible beneath his swooping bangs. In an era when most male teachers had crew cuts, his hair looked too much like ours to suggest much of an age gap.

This thin young professional, obviously straight out of student teaching, relished the title "coach" more than "teacher," and worked hard to present an image of maturity and control. He wore a tie, stood tall, adopted a commanding voice, and aspired to precisely implement the techniques presented in his classroom-management course.

This pseudo-maturity rendered him cute to the senior girls and no real testosterone threat to the adolescent boys. Most students overlooked his inexperience and appreciated his sometimes extraordinary efforts to gain our favor. We, too, went to great lengths to present ourselves as emerging young adults.

We even did our best to oblige Coach Price's request to be in our seats for roll call, but high school seniors can define "in seats" in so many different ways. Some stood beside their chair with a foot on the lower rail, while others merely steadied themselves by leaning forward with both hands on the chair-back. Others actually sat in their chairs, though not all faced forward. Some straddled their chairs, facing away from Coach Price to continue conversations with friends closer to the rear.

A loud and persistent rap on the closed classroom door gained our attention more effectively than young Coach Price had ever managed. The sharp pounding obviously came from more than the typical four knuckles used as a gentle announcement of one's presence. The distinct tone of metal on metal also ruled out the kick of a sneaker or the blunt underside of a clenched fist.

Coach Price, standing taller than usual, marched to the door with a pace and purpose designed for the approval of the thirty young critics now watching his every move. He swung the door inward and inquired, "May I help you?"

An unfamiliar black student with an impressive five-inch afro took a step into the classroom, crowding Coach Price's position. The young teacher retreated half a step, then remembered the classroom-management lesson about standing one's ground.

Before Coach Price could regain his full composure, the intruder calmly stated, "I need Adam Cherry." Coach Price rotated his upper body without giving more ground and looked at me quizzically.

I looked back curiously, noting that while the rap on the door had been loud and impressive, Coach Price wasn't evidencing any anxiety beyond his everyday first-year teacher jitters. The student visitor didn't look particularly menacing, standing quietly with both hands behind his back, rocking forward gently.

As a 185-pound high school linebacker with strong

aspirations to play college football, I was pretty accurate in assessing weight. I pegged Coach Price at 5'9" and 160. With the visitor standing so close to Coach Price, it was easy to see he was a couple of inches taller, and a good 20 pounds heavier—in fact, about my size, I surmised.

I read the visitor's bland expression as an indication that he was a messenger sent by an authority figure somewhere in the building. Maybe those tardy slips were actually being recorded by Coach Price, and Vice-Principal Massey had summoned me for a discussion.

I left my seat, three desks from the front row, and moved across the room toward the door. As self-conscious teenagers do, I realized that my saunter across the front of the room was in full view of my peers. Accordingly, I slowed my pace, swaggered a bit, and made certain the elastic band of my letter jacket was pulled down over the top of my jeans.

As Coach Price returned to his desk to resume calling the roll, and I did my fashion-runway walk, the messenger stood quietly, just inside the door. I planned my next move: brushing past him in a show of dominance before following him down the hall in friendly conversation.

As I neared him, his torso suddenly twisted to the right, and there followed a fierce, wide-arcing arm-swing in the direction of my head. Glimpsing a shining object a few inches in front of his rapidly approaching fist, I instinctively extended my left forearm while thrusting my head backward, away from the action.

My forearm made contact with his just above our wrists,

stopping the forward motion of his arm. The shiny object, a silver buckle attached to a belt wrapped around his hand, gained speed, while the sling-shot action of his arm stopped abruptly. The buckle skimmed past the tip of my nose and, missing its target, continued on the path now locked in by the position of our extended forearms, contacting the kid's left cheek just below his eye. Blood immediately splattered on the pristine fabric of my cherished letter jacket.

Fear-induced adrenalin, combined with rising anger over the sudden desecration of my prized possession, created an unfamiliar rage in me. I was known for aggressive defensive play on the football field, but that was inspired by competition and status seeking. This was raw, uncontrollable emotion.

As his head recoiled from the buckle, I threw a roundhouse right hook that landed solidly on his skull just above his left temple, sending a sharp pain shooting through my knuckles and into the palm of my hand. The seconds that followed brought a flurry of flailing fists from both of us. I couldn't tell, nor do I remember, if any of our efforts landed, much less caused damage.

Suddenly, two strong arms bear-hugged me from behind. With my arms now pinned to my sides, my assailant landed a solid blow that fattened my upper lip. He followed this up with a swift kick aimed at my groin. I instinctively raised my knee up and across my torso, averting a direct hit on his target, but creating painful shin-to-shin contact.

Coach Price suddenly approached my attacker from behind and embraced him in a bear hug. I had assumed I was being restrained by the kid's accomplice, but suddenly realized that Coach Thomas' cheek was against my left ear.

The halt in action allowed me to hear Coach Thomas' gentle rhythmic urging, "Hey, hey, hey there! Come on now, calm down, calm down."

Thomas, a stout 34-year-old African-American, was my linebacker coach and athletic role model. A chiseled physique had served him well as an all-conference linebacker and fullback at the historically black Southern University in New Orleans. His dark skin and powerful moves had earned him the nickname "Night Train." We all knew it, and the black kids on the football team used it regularly with affection. Sometimes they shouted down the halls in his direction, "Night Train, Wooo, Wooo!" making a motion as if pulling the chain on a train whistle. Coach Thomas never reacted.

None of the white athletes dared utter the moniker out loud. Labels of any kind were a tricky thing at our newly integrated school. While "Night Train" seemed innocuous enough and was ever cool, racial implications and undertones were easily assumed and the most innocent statements misinterpreted. The white kids either revered or feared Coach Thomas and would never risk a slur. The black kids called their friends and meaningful adults in their lives whatever they pleased—including the "n" word. But white kids who used the "n" word in public were already attending the private schools that had popped up with the initiation of forced busing. Granted, there were a few bigots at Washington High, but they were silent bigots.

As I struggled that day against Coach Thomas' firm grip, finding myself unable to calm down, my only thoughts were to continue retaliating for the unprovoked attack. Struggling as well, my assailant shouted, "Nobody calls me that! Let that white cracker go so I can whip his honky ass!"

Without notice or warning, Coach Thomas abruptly released my arms. I immediately landed two solid blows, a quick left and overhead right, directly to my attacker's mouth and nose, with no thought or worry about the unfairness of the scene. More blood splattered.

Just as quickly as I was released, I was back under constraint, but a firm grip was no longer required. The opportunity for uncontested violence had somehow purged my anger and fear-driven rage. I stood trembling with my arms limp at my sides, Coach Thomas's arms draped loosely around mine. Surprisingly, Coach Price and my sparring partner stood opposite us in nearly the same state.

We glared at each other a bit but exchanged no words as the coaches released us. The kid bent over to retrieve his belt, blood dripping profusely from the gash it had left on his cheek. Coach Thomas moved to him quickly, placing a nurturing arm around his shoulder while carefully examining his wound. To me, this seemingly sincere compassion was confusing. Hadn't he just encouraged me to pummel this guy?

Coach Thomas spoke gently, almost whispering, as he told the young man that he might need a stitch or two. Steadying the kid, with his arm still around his back as they walked away down the hall, he led him into the gymnasium locker room to clean him up and soothe his wounds. Later, I would learn that the boy was seen by the school nurse and subsequently taken for stitches.

In today's world, both of us would have been rightfully expelled from school, with blemishes on our academic records that would never be expunged, but this was 1973 at Booker T. Washington High School. Forced integration was in its fourth year, and race relations, while improving, were still not great. Permanently expelling students for fighting would have resulted in a very small graduating class. Fights occurred often, though not quite daily. This one, however, was pretty extreme and would have had serious consequences. Yet the coaches involved never reported it, and the school nurse handled it confidentially. I was grateful for the reprieve.

My lip looked like a badly administered collagen injection, my hand was equally swollen, and there was blood on my clothes. Coach Price suggested that I head to the restroom and clean up as much as possible. My letter jacket was ruined, and blood was spattered over my jeans and new leather desert-boots. As upset as I was about the condition of my clothes and my throbbing hand, I was more concerned about the perception of me as a racist.

I held my hand under the soothing water for as long as I could, racking my brain trying to understand how the skinny kid with the belt got the impression that I hated blacks, or even just him. The water cooled the swelling heat in my hand, but did little to help me understand the turn of events that led to the unprovoked assault.

Most of the white kids at Booker T. Washington, representing 15 percent of the school population, had decided to attend the formerly all-black school because they were pro-integration. We tried hard every day to contribute to a positive transition in a rapidly changing school and a rapidly changing South. I was proud to be at Booker T. Washington, and was prepared to defend the honor of all of my fellow students with the same vigor that any red-blooded American would defend his hometown high school classmates. The assailant's allegation that I had used a racial slur—I assumed the "n" word—hurt more than my lip or my hand.

Did he really think I called him the "n" word? To be honest, I would sometimes use the word in my mind when I saw particularly outrageous behavior by a fellow student. My mental labeling, like that used by my black friends, was not targeted at any particular race, but at silly behavior that called someone's judgment into question. I would never have called that kid a "n." How did he mistake me for someone who would?

I missed my first period class, spending almost an hour soothing the rising heat in my hand under the cool running water in the bathroom sink. I couldn't, however, wash off the fight. It consumed me. When I finally reentered the halls, classmates approached, eager to probe for details.

"Did he really have a belt wrapped around his hand?"

"How'd it hit him in the face?"

"Did Night Train really let you go?"

It was easy to be pleased by the attention. Student lore judges winners and losers of school fights, and I was proud to be the winner. The unique involvement of two young and popular coaches added additional intrigue and elevated the importance of the win.

I was still pondering the bizarre event as I prepared for football practice that day. I used an ACE bandage to gently wrap my hand, hoping it would suffice for practice and go unnoticed by the trainers. Heading onto the field, I saw Coach Thomas for the first time since the morning incident. He looked me in the eye, silent and expressionless. As our shoulders passed, he reached back to give a single open-handed pat on the back of my pads, his signature acknowledgement of a job well done. Coach Thomas was always subtle, nonverbal, and stingy with his praise. I was relieved and fortified by his response.

Football practice was always strenuous. Like most of my teammates, I loved the game but hated practice. With calisthenics and one-on-one tackling drills out of the way, we moved quickly into the only enjoyable part of practice, the first-team defense scrimmaging against the second-team offense. Many of us on the first-team defense were also members of the second-team offense, which meant we were mostly scrimmaging against younger and inexperienced third-string players.

Early in the scrimmage, I failed to retreat into pass coverage on the appropriate cue and was burned by a 15-yard pass caught by a scrawny sophomore receiver named

Joe Johnson. I sheepishly glanced toward Coach Thomas. He was looking in my general direction but didn't comment. I knew the lack of reaction in no way condoned the mistake.

Resolved to make amends, I watched the skinny black receiver break from the huddle and head for the left side of the field, setting up as a flanker slightly off the line of scrimmage, just outside the shoulder of the tight end. I eagerly assumed my position as the weak-side linebacker on the opposite side of the ball, immediately recognizing an alignment that would likely be used by our Friday night opponent. Earlier in the week, Coach Thomas had shown us this configuration and the three or four plays it would produce.

At the snap, my job was to look through the offensive tackle into the backfield to discern whether it would be a pass or run. If I detected pass, I was supposed to retreat into the right side flat. I didn't bother to make my read. My eyes were on the little receiver, who at the snap dashed forward with the big tight end. As I anticipated, and as he was instructed, the flanker broke behind the larger player and headed in my direction on a short crossing route over the middle. The third-string quarterback was watching him intently from the snap. It didn't take a seasoned senior to figure out to whom he would throw.

I abandoned my right-side responsibilities, calculating a collision course. The quarterback waited until the middle linebacker followed the big tight end away from his target and tossed a slow, wobbly pass that split the rapidly closing space between me and the receiver. Joe's eyes were intently focused on the floating ball. Mine were fixed on the space between the 8 and 4 on his jersey. He reached high for the barely catchable ball, never sensing my intentions.

The facemask part of my helmet made contact with his chest just above the numbers and slid along an upward path into his chin. His feet continued their forward momentum as his head recoiled and headed in the opposite direction. My feet never left the ground as I ran right through him. Straddling my teammate, I peered down into his helmet to see his mouth bleeding and his eyes blurry slits.

The hoots and hollers of my first-team defensive teammates filled the air, but I was uncertain how to respond, looking straight down into Joe's questioning eyes. Before I could sort through my emotions, four burly black fingers thrust through the center of my facemask and my eyes were violently jerked up and away from Joe.

I was suddenly face to face with Coach Thomas. His huge Popeye-like forearm quivered from his intense grasp on my facemask. Bending over between me and the downed player, he screamed so ferociously that a hush enveloped the open field.

"Who the hell do you think you are, you sorry little piece of crap?"

Admiring teammates were suddenly silent. Other coaches and trainers ran in our direction as his rant continued.

"What makes you think that bull-crap is football? Gutless cheap shots have no place on my field!" he yelled directly into my facemask. Despite my averted gaze, I caught a glimpse of the throbbing blue-black artery on the side of his neck as splatters of spit passed through the protective mask onto my face.

"Where the hell were you supposed to be on that play? Sure as hell not here!" he finished, releasing my facemask as quickly as he had grabbed it. Disgusted, he turned away to attend to Joe.

His emotions quickly switched from rage to compassionate concern as he squatted down and gently unsnapped Joe's chinstrap, careful not to move his head before any spinal damage could be assessed. His last action toward me was to forcefully shove his forearm into my thigh pad, knocking me awkwardly off balance and out of the dominant straddling position I continued to hold over my teammate.

Disappointment turned to shame as I stood alone on the sideline, having been immediately and permanently replaced in the scrimmage. Teammates stayed far away lest they be implicated in some way. Joe Johnson, the injured sophomore, had a split chin that wouldn't require stitches, but he was removed from the scrimmage as a precaution against a possible concussion. While relieved that he wasn't seriously hurt, I was, selfishly, more concerned about the damage done to my relationship with Coach Thomas.

I moved away from the group of coaches and trainers attending to the injured Joe, trying not to draw attention to myself. I wasn't just instantly deflated, I was totally distraught. My role model was now as disgusted with me as he'd been proud earlier in the day.

Every football practice ended with obligatory wind sprints. As I slowed to cross the last line on the final sprint, Coach Thomas blocked my path and pointed down toward the line. His intentions were clear; I wasn't finished running. During the following thirty minutes of additional sprinting, he never said a word—just blew his whistle every time I dragged myself to the line and changed direction.

That Friday night, when the official lineup was released, I wasn't listed as a starter, but was inserted into the game in the second half. No explanation was given. In fact, Coach Thomas never mentioned either incident from earlier in the week.

Joe Johnson, eager to be accepted by his older teammates, held no apparent grudge. I was pleased and relieved when he got onto the field with under two minutes in the game and caught his first pass, over the middle. We won an easy game over an inferior opponent.

I never again saw the belt-swinging kid, and never confirmed his motive. School lore continued to frame the fight as racial. A black kid constrained by a white coach while I, the white kid, was only partially held back by a black coach couldn't be defined as anything less. In truth, adolescent fights between and across races were common with the slightest provocation, or misperception of provocation, quickly leading to blows. I've relived that day over and over in my mind for decades.

As a high school football player with grand, professional

football aspirations—none of which would be realized, I might add—I perceived Coach Thomas as the poster child of "tough." Like the rest of my teammates, I feared his every move and followed his every suggestion. His powerful physique, commanding presence, and understated demeanor were perfectly suited to inspire the disciplined aggression required of a great defensive football player. I longed to look and act like Coach Thomas.

In retrospect, Coach Thomas was much more than a coach to me. He understood the complexities of the time and was the poster child for justice and compassion in an often unjust and aggressive world. He never spoke to us of race or injustice, nor did he try to explain his views about physical aggression or compassion. Rather, he chose to immerse himself in an environment that every day provided numerous opportunities to act—actions that would be closely monitored and interpreted by scores of adoring and malleable young people.

That morning, Coach Thomas took action based upon what he knew of the situation at the time. A kid shows up at a classroom door and swings a belt, then continues to admonish his target after being restrained. His view of restoring justice included letting me go for a few more punches. He could, and should, be seriously questioned for his violence-condoning tactics, and in today's world, would have been fired on the spot.

Later that day, he reinforced the message. Unprovoked aggression is unprovoked aggression. My decision to use force on a defenseless, unsuspecting peer was no more appropriate than my assailant's actions towards me earlier in the day.

Unexpectedly, the gruff and burly coach repeatedly demonstrated that even when emotions run high and egregious acts have been committed, compassion is necessary for restoration. He repeatedly demonstrated his concern for the well-being of those caught up in behaviors with potentially harmful outcomes.

Coach Thomas taught these complex lessons of restoration to countless students—sometimes with a fist, sometimes with a warm towel, sometimes with cold water, and sometimes with wind sprints.

ASPIRATION

CHAPTER THREE

It'll be hours before I can accurately assess the severity of Eugene's laminitis. The vet could undoubtedly do it quickly, but calling a vet would be expensive and take more precious time from my piddle day.

Furthermore, a prognosis from a vet will void all excuses for not calling Betty with the news. As long as there are questions about the severity of the problem, it's premature to communicate that there is one. I try to convince myself of this, wondering if every husband whose marriage has survived for three decades has developed this level of sophistication in carefully orchestrating the timing and necessity of communication. It's not that I'm afraid to tell her. Actually, I am, but why bother worrying her with what, in the end, might turn out to be a non-problem?

Above the tack room door, the playful plastic clock across from Eugene's stall announces 8:00 a.m. with a horse's head darting through a stall door and a loud whinny. We've accumulated an extraordinary amount of horse-related paraphernalia in the short time we've been living on the farm.

I enter his stall one more time to hand-check the temperature of his back hooves. Is it just wishful thinking, or are they a bit cooler after forty-five minutes of cold water hosing in the wash rack? Healing takes time, I remind myself.

The nine other horses, including my own sweet Nellie, aren't used to so much activity in the barn this early, particularly before receiving their morning grain and hay. At first, they stand by quietly and watch the unfamiliar activity in the wash rack. I even read into their reactions a bit of concern for Eugene. But they adjust quickly to the novelty of the situation and are soon noisily expressing discontent with the breakfast delay.

I head back to the feed room knowing that the horses' patience will further wane and that the noise level will increase exponentially when I re-open the lid to the feed bin. Fortunately, I extracted Eugene with just enough grain left for the others to have breakfast. It won't be enough for dinner, but there'll be plenty of time to make it to the feed store. I make a mental note that it's Sunday and the store will be open from one to five.

Remembering the cuckoo horse's announcement of the hour, I sigh in recognition that I have already burned hours of my precious day on totally unanticipated events. Many dads are still enjoying their slumber or at least being served breakfast in bed. I've douched a dog and nursed a horse with a mouth bigger than his stomach, and I have less and less time left for piddling.

The horses are loud and either pacing in circles or nervously moving their heads back and forth ("weaving") at their stall door, occasionally expressing their impatience with a neigh. I begin placing carefully prescribed amounts of grain and various supplements into individualized buckets.

The dogs are no less hungry than the horses, but the horses express their hunger with more serious potential consequences. When food is expected but is slow in being delivered, the dogs whine and wag their tails vigorously. Once in a while, they even abandon their training and rise onto their back legs to put their front paws on the thighs of an inattentive potential feeder. The horses, in contrast, rear, kick violently at the sides of their stall, chew the edges of their feeders, and whinny to one another at a volume and pitch that could wake the distant neighbors.

Each of the horses in our care has a slightly different morning diet. Some get more grain than others in an effort to influence their weight or to appease a delicate digestive system. Most get some sort of supplement, purportedly to put sheen on their coat, reduce swelling in their joints, or simply calm them down a bit. As a group, horses are big, high-strung, and delicate creatures.

I feed those depending upon me for food: ten horses, two dogs, six barn cats, and God only knows how many fish.

The cats are mousers and only get a little supplemental food lest they lose motivation to perform their real job. Truth be told, the cats are the only animals I feed that have a "real job." Theoretically, the horses need to be well-fed in order to do their job—carrying or pulling people and things. Most horses, however, lost their "real job" status with the invention of the combustion engine.

While the horses at our place are ridden, the rides are for leisure, not transportation. From this perspective, the horses are no more necessary than the dogs. For that matter, if we didn't have the horses, we wouldn't need a barn, which would mean we wouldn't have to worry about mice in the barn, which would mean that the cats wouldn't have a real job either.

The fish in the pond? Same.

The small pond next to the barn is loaded with blue gill and largemouth bass. I feed them their own special grain each morning and catch them in the evening. Theoretically, they could be a food source and in this way have a real job, but I admire the fight that ensues when they realize the evening worm on the hook doesn't go down as effortlessly as the morning grain. That admiration, combined with an environmentalist friend's detailed explanation of the carcinogens they could potentially have absorbed from farm fertilizer run-off, easily convinces me that throwing them back to be caught another day is the best course of action. One day, however, when it least expects it, a fish will fulfill its life's work.

The bottom line is that the animals on the farm, and the farm itself, are largely unnecessary. They serve no real purpose beyond fulfilling our lifelong, now fully embraced, dream.

We've purposefully chosen this lifestyle, and all of the animals have become part of it. The dogs, horses, cats, and fish generate the bulk of both work and enjoyment. They're periodically joined by a host of wild critters who play important support roles.

I regularly curse the deer for eating the flowers at dusk and vow to find clever ways of keeping them off of the farm. Yet the same deer leave me paralyzed with worry that I will frighten them away when they stand majestically in the pasture during the early morning mist. The squirrels, opossum, rabbits, raccoons, coyotes—and, of course, the skunks—entertain us and intrigue us with their unique evolutionary survival strategies. Some run, some hide, some deceive, some spray, some fight.

Together, we all provide the farm with purpose, creating a place where we thrive and benefit from each other's presence. Our dreams for the farm are derived from this purpose, and each project is derived from these dreams.

The horses will one day thrive when I plow-under the grass currently covering the back-seven acres and replace it with lush alfalfa. We will then enjoy Eugene and Nellie's shinier coats as they graze happily in the field. A large new fountain in the pond will one day aerate the water conditions for the fish, reduce the algae, and create beautiful sights and sounds for all to enjoy. New black, four-rail fencing and cross-fencing will contain those who need to be contained, separate those who need separating, and let others move freely across the property.

Dreams for the property and the new projects they create are exciting and endless. Yet, these improvements seem perpetually delayed by the more mundane day-to-day realities of farm life. One of those daily realities faces me now. Stall cleaning!

Spoiled Nellie is always first out of the barn. I enter her stall and carefully place a bright blue halter over her striped forehead and behind her ears, then latch it under her neck. A blue lead-line clips easily to the metal halter loop just under her chin. I walk her through the barn and out into the front pasture.

The other horses take as much note of this activity as they did the distribution of grain. They whinny and neigh, requesting that they be next to go out onto the green pasture grass. Like impatient guests at a well-stocked buffet line, they all know they will get their turn but want to be at the head of the line nonetheless.

Star and Prissy are pleasantly surprised to be joining Nellie in the lush front pasture, a privilege usually reserved for Eugene, whose recent transgressions will keep him inside today. Nellie enjoys Star and Prissy's company nearly as much as Eugene's.

With Nellie, Star, and Prissy out front, I lead Lacy and Pepper, the remaining mares, to one of the back pastures. The geldings have waited somewhat patiently and, within a few more minutes, Zach, Apollo, Mohito, and Macho Man are all out in the other back-pasture. Eugene remains in solitary confinement in the barn.

The horses typically stay out in the pasture during the day and return to their stalls for dinner, a good night's rest, and breakfast. As you might imagine, two full meals and over 14 hours in a stall generate substantial manure and wet bedding.

Reentering Nellie's stall, I begin removing manure with a long stall pick, which is a modern plastic iteration of the old metal pitchfork. Using the bright-orange, fork-like pick with ten 8" tongs spaced an inch apart, I am able to remove the manure along with the sawdust bedding wet from frequent and impressive urination.

I place the "muck" in twenty gallon buckets, filling two buckets from Nellie's stall alone. Similar amounts of muck are generated in each of the remaining nine stalls.

Farmers measure dry goods in bushels. The muck's not dry but relatively solid. Nonetheless, my suburban mentality still has me thinking in gallons. The buckets hold nearly 18 gallons of muck, which I've learned translates into 2 bushels. That's 20 bushels—180 gallons—of muck each day. That's 7,300 bushels, or 65,700 gallons, a year. Simply put, it's a mountain of crap.

What does one do with that much crap?

When we first saw the advertisement for the farm we would eventually purchase, we were amused by the line, "manure spreader included." At first, we thought it was in some way referring to the realtor we would encounter. After a few weeks on the farm, its value as a sales feature became much more obvious, as did its function.

Manure spreaders spread manure. They are basically a large poop bin on wheels designed to throw muck in all directions when pulled by a tractor across a field.

Our spreader holds 100 bushels of muck and is "ground driven." That is, as the wheels turn, a series of attached gears and chains begin to slowly push the pile of muck toward the opening at the back of the container where the "beaters" are mounted.

The beaters, also turned by gears attached to the wheels, are rapidly spinning pieces of metal of various shapes and sizes which collide with the manure as it moves toward the back opening of the bin as it's pulled across the field. The result is horse poop flying in all directions, but eventually spread evenly across the field.

As gross as it sounds, a functioning manure spreader is essential to a horse farm's operation. The lack of a spreader means piling manure close enough to the barn that the muck buckets can be emptied directly onto the pile. Such a pile can be distributed later, or given away to neighbors who value the excrement as garden fertilizer. However, the smell and flies generated by the pile make it highly undesirable to keep around for any length of time.

The 30-year-old spreader we inherited is functional but not pretty, not that any manure spreader would be labeled pretty by anyone other than a diehard horse farmer. However, the ones at the feed store are built of shiny red metal with matching white-walled tires and shiny hitches. Ours has slightly rotting wood sideboards with severely flaking John Deere green paint. Every piece of metal is rust brown, and none of the tires match in size, color, or shape.

Nonetheless, it spreads poop well. I pull it using our tractor of about the same vintage and of nearly the same condition. They match, and together they get the job done.

At optimum speed for spreading, the poop flies ten feet into the air and ends up evenly distributed across a wide swath of the field. It's a beautiful thing!

I dump Nellie's muck into the old spreader and notice that it's been a few days since it was emptied. It should hold the eighteen muck buckets from the nine remaining stalls, but no more.

One-by-one, I clean each of the other nine stalls, filling two muck buckets in each stall and emptying them into the manure spreader before moving on to the next. At almost ten minutes per stall, it takes an hour and a half to complete the job.

My capacity estimate turns out to be a bit optimistic. The last two buckets had to be dumped with great care to keep the chunks of poop from rolling down and over the sides of the spreader. The result is a wagon load of manure that's more than ready to be spread.

But wait! The tractor always seems to be hitched to an implement other than the one that's necessary for the task at hand. Today's no different. The tractor is hooked to the drag that I use to level and condition the riding surface in the arena. I unhook the drag and move the tractor around to connect it to the spreader. The 26-horse-power tractor is small but properly geared down to be quite powerful. It struggles a bit in adequately powering the hay baler but has no trouble pulling the spreader.

I pull the spreader to the back of the hay field before stopping, dismounting the tractor, and pulling the lever on the front of the spreader that engages the wheels to move the bars, that churn the chains, that push the manure toward the spinning metal shapes, that cause the manure to be flung wildly through the air.

Watching the manure fly reminds me of chaotic exchanges with colleagues whose only purpose is to spread big words in random patterns such that, in the end, they're equally distributed across the minutes of a meeting.

As I ponder this analogy, the poop suddenly stops flying.

The tractor is still moving. The spreader is still perfectly connected. The metal shapes are still rotating. But the poop's not flying! I'm depressed to see that a full three-quarters of the manure remains in the spreader.

Fearing the worst, I shut down the old diesel motor and listen to it spit and sputter to a stop. I dismount once again and, before I get close enough to peer inside the spreader, identify the problem. A ten-foot section of chain hangs from the back of the spreader and stretches across the field. Before the chain broke, it was strategically located in the spreader and doing its job pushing the manure toward the rotating blades. Now, it's merely a sign that even more of my precious day is going to be wasted.

Seasoned horse farmers know that one rule of the farm is that manure spreaders never break when empty.

Today, I'm fortunate that it's June and the manure is only hot and full of flies. Emptying the spreader will be a filthy and tiring job, but manageable. In January, frozen manure inside of a broken spreader means starting a pile next to the barn and continuing to fill it until the spring thaw, when the spreader can be emptied and fixed.

I walk through the hay field, then traverse the back pasture toward the shed to retrieve a shovel. Lola and Bo shy away from the tractor and spreader when the poop is flying, but welcome the opportunity to join me in a walk through the hay field. They run in front, bouncing rhythmically through the tall grass, reminding me of dolphins cresting the water and then disappearing below.

The cell phone in my pocket emits a short, loud beep as I'm walking. Taking it from my pocket, I see a second missed call and message. It must have rung while I was driving the noisy tractor. This being Father's Day, I'll be excused for some delay in returning calls, but I'm smart enough to know there's a limit. One of the first things I'll be asked is: "When did you get my message?"

It's such a double-edged question. Admitting that I listened to the message early in the day and didn't call back is problematic. Admitting that I didn't bother to listen to the message might be worse. Even though it's one's special day, there's always proper protocol. Given that it's mid-morning, I push the button with the phone icon, intending to listen to the two messages. Before the first message can play, the phone goes dead. The battery's shot, and this isn't good. The phone goes right back in my pocket.

Now, more problems.

The shovel's not in the shed where it should be. I quietly wish that I had someone to blame for misplaced tools, but

I realize, all too well, that I'm the last person to have used the shovel. I finally find it next to the worm bed, created for convenience beside the fish pond.

With shovel in hand, I walk the half mile back to the tractor at the end of the hay field and, already dripping sweat, climb into the bed of the spreader. There's just enough room from where the distributed manure once sat for me to get my boots squarely positioned on the wood surface of the spreader floor—the best position to shovel out 13 or so bushels of crap. The flies enjoy my company in the spreader as much as the dogs did in the hay field.

Nearly an hour later, the spreader is empty and I'm a hot, stinking mess. I pull the broken chain back into the bed of the empty spreader. Given that this is not my first chain break, I know how to fix it. But I also know that it's a two-hour job, assuming I have the necessary parts and that all goes perfectly—two major assumptions.

I pull the manure spreader to the rear of the barn, realizing that I could spend the remainder of the day twisting chains and banging on connector parts. It is almost 11:00 a.m. and my dream day spent alone on the farm is rapidly turning into a nightmare.

As always, the parts you need are the hardest to find. The chain parts are stored in the very back corner of the shed behind the barn. As I reposition tools to reach the replacement chains for the spreader, I'm forced to move a different type of chain-holding device—the chain saw. The sight of the saw reminds me of some piddling I'd planned.

I've always pictured a special bench out by the pond; a bench with a simple sturdy design, but one that represents the character and self-sufficiency of the place. All I need is a sharp chain and a property full of logs. Having both, it's just a matter of prioritizing the time.

Picking up the saw and noting that it's full of gas and oil, I decide that my obligation to fix the manure spreader will have to wait. On the second pull of the cord, the blue smoke and roaring motor confirm the saw is operational. I shut it down immediately, leave the shed, and walk back to the tractor. Unhooking it from the spreader, I feel no guilt about not fixing it, but place the saw in the bucket of the tractor's front end loader and head toward the wooded property-line out back.

Last month's wind storm left plenty of work for the saw—two large oak trees were overturned at their roots. I scout out the downed trees, and it doesn't take long to find the three pieces I'll need for the bench: two short chunks of trunk for the base, and a long straight piece for the seat, all about 14 inches in diameter. The base pieces don't need to be much more than a foot long.

The sharp saw makes quick work of the largest section of downed trunk and produces eerily identical logs. Cutting equal size logs is the easy part. Cutting a side-to-side, U-shaped notch on the top of each log is a bit more challenging, but still doesn't require lumberjack-level talent.

The bench top I had in mind would be about four feet long and uniformly round, with just a few limbs. A few removed limbs would leave knots to add character. Too many would be unsightly. There's ample trunk on the ground, and I quickly find, and cut, a perfect length.

I set the base pieces next to one another with the U-notches forming a continuous cradle. The top log fits perfectly in the cradle, with one end extending two feet beyond the bases. Now for the tricky part, the part requiring a very steady hand. I rev the saw and begin slicing the top piece of log down the middle. When the saw reaches the first base, I shut it down, flip the log around, and start from the other end. The plan is to reach the middle from both ends with a perfectly aligned cut such that the two sides fall apart in identically-sized pieces.

Halfway through the first cut, my aim drifts off center and the piece is ruined. Refusing to give up on my dream, I find another section of trunk, almost as perfect as the first, and start over. This time, the two pieces split perfectly. As they fall apart, I realize for the first time that I have the natural makings of two benches, not one. I methodically cut and notch another set of identical bases. With the tractor bucket loaded down, I head back to the pond.

My vision for the bench placed it strategically behind the fire pit so that I could sit and look through the fire across the entire pond. Now, I'll have to adjust that vision so that two benches can be placed at perfect angles to produce the same view for sitters, while also allowing those seated to see each other and carry on a conversation. I arrange the bases and finish the job by simply putting the top half-log into the notches. No posts in the ground, and no nails—just a simple, sturdy bench.

The benches look just as I envisioned them. I sit on one, admiring the other, and an irresistible urge overcomes me. Grabbing the saw, I approach the newly-cut surface of one bench and use the very tip to carve the initials "BC" a quarter of an inch deep in the center. I move directly to the other bench and add, "AC." His and Her benches for Betty and Adam Cherry.

Wednesday, October 11, 1987

Pat held the ladder and verbally directed my movements toward the prize.

"Just to your right," he instructed. "A little higher." Then, "That's it, that's the one. What a beauty!"

As I gently pulled the shiny apple from its stem on the loaded fruit tree, he added rhetorically, "Not a worm hole in it, is there?" I inspected the apple and had to agree. It was perfect.

I'd been on the ladder for over 20 minutes, having been aimed and positioned by Pat, who was on the ground, to pick each apple for what was becoming a very full bucket. All of the apples in the tree looked perfect to me, and the overburdened branches were begging to be picked, but Pat had a clear and unwavering vision of what a perfect, full bucket of apples should look like and which specific apples would fulfill his vision. I suspected that he'd been scouting the apples for weeks before my arrival in anticipation of this well-planned "picking party."

There was also no doubt that he had a clear idea of the process we'd use to turn the scrumptious fruit into applesauce. The first five years of marriage had taught me that my father-in-law always had a plan.

With the bucket full, he helped me down the ladder. We replaced it in the shed and headed back into the house. Pat and Joanne, my in-laws, purchased the semi-wooded six acres on the northern California hillside just after Betty and I were married. The house needed some work, but the view of the valley below more than justified the effort. It quickly became the center of their lives.

Back in the house, the second phase of Pat's applesauce plan was revealed. Walking into the kitchen, I focused my attention on an unfamiliar shiny contraption mounted on the front edge of the tile countertop just beside the sink: a red handle attached to a six-inch piece of metal. The device already held a perfect apple, and it didn't take a mechanical engineer to recognize it as an apple peeler.

"Can you guess what that is?" Pat asked, obviously pleased with my quizzical look. The confirmation that I had never seen or used an apple peeler only made the well-planned applesauce-making exercise more special for him.

Pat walked over to the device and gave the crank a quick, full turn. The apple spun symmetrically around the post on which it was mounted. The cutting device, loaded with a spring to create constant pressure, smoothly removed one full ring of skin from the turning apple. Pat stepped back and motioned with his hand for me to take up the work as if he were offering first passage to a magical destination.

"It's all yours," he said with pride.

His tone implied that not only would I get to experience the tool and the applesauce it would produce, but apparently I now owned an apple peeler.

I moved past Pat and assumed the task of turning the crank. About seven revolutions later, the apple was completely naked, and the skin lay in ringlets on the counter. I removed the apple from the device and was surprised to see that the simple rotations had not only sliced the apple with a spiral effect, but completely removed its core. The apple peeler was indeed a simple and elegant tool that I would welcome into a growing arsenal of kitchen weapons.

"Well, look at that!" I exclaimed to Pat's delight.

"Thanks so much," I added without looking up, continuing to inspect the nifty machine.

Years later, I would learn that Pat introduced this very same process to each of his other three sons-in-law, and that later he would do the same with his grandchildren as they came of applesauce-making age. Indeed, it was a clever way to gift an object that Pat was convinced most fruit lovers required.

The remainder of the applesauce-making process was unexceptional. The peeled and sliced apples ended up in a pot with a bit of butter, brown sugar, and cinnamon. A little heat, a few stirs, and about 20 minutes later we were eating fresh applesauce. Not mushy sauce like that bought at the grocery store, but mouth-watering apple sauce with soft yet distinct chunks of apple.

The applesauce itself was great, but I had to surmise it was no better than the same homemade stuff I'd seen in jars filling the top row of my in-laws' pantry. Was it great simply because it contained the freshest of ingredients? Or was it the effort that created a self-fulfilling prophecy? For Pat, it was irrelevant. Fulfillment was in the experience, not the product.

We ate the applesauce for breakfast along with several dried fruits from the same orchard. It was late fall, and apples were the last fresh fruit of the year, but Pat was a master at preserving each harvest. Pears, peaches, or plums—it didn't matter how many grew or when they ripened. Some were dried, some made it into preserves, and others seemed to have a miraculous shelf-life, strategically placed in baskets in the dark garage.

"I'm done with chickens," he suddenly proclaimed, followed by an apology for not having fresh eggs to accompany our morning fruit. He then related the trials and tribulations of trying to keep the fox out of the hen house over the past five years. After dozens of sacrificial offerings of fowl to fox, he explained, he had given up on maintaining laying hens.

Pat had learned a lot in the five years since moving from a suburban neighborhood to the property just outside of town, but he had decided that he couldn't beat the sly fox. I surmised that fresh eggs weren't a critical part of his grand dream for "Mountain View Ranch." If eggs had been central to his dream, I would have changed my bet from the fox to

Pat.

My in-laws called the six acres a ranch, but it would never house horse or cattle. Goats were acquired now and again, but eventually were deemed an unbearable nuisance because they were constantly wiggling through the holes in the antiquated wire fencing, finding the grass always greener on the neighbor's side. Eventually, two special dogs and a feral cat were the only domestic animals on the property. There were, however, thousands of other living things that required their care—green growing things.

Pat had a passion for plants and an amazing green thumb, despite perpetual northern California water shortages. In fact, the semi-arid land high on the hill should have been labeled Mountain View Nursery. He acquired plants by the dozens and added hundreds as his dream abode came to fruition.

Pat and I were alone this morning on the six acres. Betty, her mom, and our children had left early in the morning to help Betty's sister prepare for the upcoming delivery of her first child—Pat and Joanne's fifth grandchild. Betty and I lived over 700 miles away with two of those grandchildren. We visited a few times each year and, when we did, there were always people to see and things to do with the large family.

Joanne invited me to join her and Betty on their quest to provide unsolicited nursery design advice to my pregnant sister-in-law. It was a tempting invitation. Not that I had the slightest interest in outfitting nurseries, but I enjoyed hitting a few tennis balls with my relatively new brother-in-law, who would inevitably be more than willing to slip away from the nursery discussions to play a set or two.

Betty pulled me aside before leaving and asked, "Can you stay here with my dad and make gumbo for tonight?"

On many occasions, Betty had raved about my gumbo to her parents, but I hadn't found time to prepare it on any of our previous action-packed trips. Her four siblings and their families were joining us for dinner, and it would be the perfect addition to the festivities.

"Sure," I replied with a twinge of disappointment at missing out on tennis.

"Great," Betty responded with a sly smile. "I got you the ingredients yesterday."

I had readily agreed, figuring I had all day to cook the gumbo and would also be able to get in some much-needed writing time. I was stressing out over the pressures of producing enough research publications to warrant tenure and a promotion to associate professor at a major research university.

Pat usually had chores that would keep him occupied, so the early morning plan was to offer enough support to gain favor with my father-in-law, then beg out of the ranch tasks with the excuse that I needed to rewrite a recently reviewed paper so I could continue to provide for his daughter and grandchildren. I would make the roux for the gumbo so that I seemed busy as I sat at the kitchen table, begrudgingly appeasing my colleagues with detailed responses to their challenging comments about my paper.

The applesauce-making activity was technically completed before breakfast. However, additional chores and Pat's attention to detail in completing them had pushed us well into the day. Breakfast ended just before 11:00 a.m. as we ceremoniously completed the washing and drying of the apple peeler and carefully placed it back in its original box.

It was later than I expected, but there was still enough time to get my gumbo done along with a few hours of productive work on the paper, which I had no choice but to revise before returning to campus.

I was preparing to convey my plans to Pat when he appeared holding a familiar flannel shirt. Before I could speak, he extended it in my direction.

"For you," he said, knowing that I recognized the shirt as the one I'd worn over my t-shirt the last time I'd visited. It was his spare planting shirt, one that could get dirty as we dug holes and transported root balls of one variety or another against our chests.

"I've got something special for you to help me with," he said with a smile.

As I tried to craft a polite demurral, he added, "I think you'll enjoy it, but we need to get it done before the others arrive . . . It won't take long."

I knew better.

I may have been relatively new to the family, but I was a quick learner. Producing Pat's "something special" surprise for the family would not be a quick task. During our visit the previous fall, when our children were three and five, we spent an entire day planting two California Redwood trees high on the hillside above my in-laws' home. The trees were only five feet or so in height, and were planted in the five-gallon buckets purchased from the nursery.

Nonetheless, an entire morning had been spent at the nursery, with each child carefully selecting their own Redwood. After we transported the trees to Mountain View Ranch, the children went inside to nap while Pat and I removed the trees from the back of his truck, placed each of them in a wheel barrow, and pushed them up the California hillside a hundred and fifty yards above their house. We then dug two holes three feet wide and two feet deep, and mixed tree planting fertilizer into each hole. We placed each tree next to its hole. Then we stopped.

Nothing with Pat was without ceremony. We waited another hour for the children to rise from their naps and join us on the hill along with their mother and grandmother. Then each child took a turn pushing their tree toward the hole with all their might, as Pat watched them adoringly and feigned a lack of strength until each child's tree was resting properly in its hole. Finally, each would use their own miniature shovel, with their name hand-whittled by their grandfather into its wooden handle, to help him fill in the space around the tree.

As precious as the exercise was in retrospect, it took all day. On that day, too, Pat had claimed, "It won't take long!"

My anxiety spiked for a moment as I considered the urgency of revising the paper, which was due back to the hyper-critical editors the next week. It spiked further when I remembered my gumbo promise and the entire family coming over to critique what would be, for them, a novelty dish.

Pat grabbed his keys and I begrudgingly followed him to the truck. As we got in, he sensed my concern about a long road trip and offered, "We only have two quick stops."

Still not convinced that we'd be back in time for me to make the gumbo, much less work on my paper, I sat quietly as we navigated down the winding half-mile drive to the canyon road. Pat took one hand off the wheel and pointed in the general direction of the old truck's glove box.

"There's something in there I want you to see."

The latch on the glove box hung a bit, but it flew open with a tug, sending a fresh white envelope to the floor. Old receipts and the original operating manual for the 20-year-old truck miraculously remained firmly embedded together. I reached down between my legs, picked up the simple business envelope, and studied its contents carefully.

Two pages of text had been typed on the old IBM Selectric that sat squarely in the center of the desk in the guest/office room in their home—it was the last of the electric typewriters.

I unfolded the pages and took a quick look at both. It was a contract of sorts, complete with lines for dated signatures. I could see Pat curiously monitoring my moves out of the corner of his eye as he continued to drive.

Mountain View Puppy Partners
Memorandum of Understanding

DATE: October 11, 1987

This agreement is between Pat May (hereinafter "Grandpa") and his five grandchildren (hereinafter "the Grandkids").

Grandpa and the Grandkids agree to create a new business, the Mountain View Puppy Partners (hereinafter "Puppy Partners"). The Puppy Partners business will raise and sell puppies with the goal of saving money for the Grandkids to use for college.

Puppy Partners will be created by October 11, 1987 and will end on October 10, 1997.

Business Plan

Puppy Partners will begin with the purchase of two puppies. Grandpa suggests that these puppies be Labrador Retrievers (hereinafter "Labs"). Grandpa's research indicates that:

- *Labs are good with children.*
- *Labs produce large litters of puppies.*
- *Labs are one of the easiest dogs to sell.*

The Grandkids can try to convince Grandpa that other breeds would be good, but Grandpa will request evidence to support this argument.

Grandpa will raise the two Lab puppies, and when they are old enough to have puppies of their own, they will be bred and have litters of puppies. The puppies from each litter will be sold to families who have children who want a puppy to love. Grandpa will collect the money from the sale of the puppies and put it in the bank, where it will earn interest. On October 11, 1997, Grandpa will:

- *Take the money out of the bank.*
- *Subtract the business expenses from the total earned from selling the puppies.*
- *Divide the money into five equal amounts.*
- *Give each of the Grandkids their share of the money to use when they go to college.*

Responsibilities for Grandpa

- *Buy two young female Lab puppies (one chocolate and one yellow so that we can tell them and their puppies apart) and raise them at Mountain View Ranch.*
- *Care for every new litter of Lab puppies. This includes feeding them, taking them to the vet, and cleaning up after them.*
- *Find a male Labrador Retriever (hereinafter "Daddy Dog") to breed to each of the female dogs when they are old enough.*
- *Sell the puppies from every new litter, making certain that Joanne May (hereinafter "Grandma") does not get too attached to the pups and want to keep one or two.*
- *Put the money from the puppy sales into the bank and*

hold for the Grandkids.

- *Write the monthly Puppy Partners Newsletter.*
- *Close the business and distribute the funds to the Grandkids.*

<u>*Responsibilities for the Grandkids*</u>

- *Earn $15.00 to invest in the business by working for your parents. Suggestions: Wash the car, rake leaves, fold clothes.*
- *Read the materials on Lab puppies and how to care for them.*
- *Name the two initial puppies.*
- *Help Grandpa predict how much money the partnership will make and how much they will get.*
- *Visit their business partner (Grandpa) and every litter of new puppies.*
- *Decide with their parents if they can have one of the puppies from one of the litters.*
- *Work with Grandpa to socialize the puppies so that they like children.*
- *Read the monthly Puppy Partner Newsletter.*
- *Go to college and spend the money for that.*

<u>*Budget*</u>

Revenue:

- *Grandchildren Investment—5 @ $15 = $75*

- *Chocolate Lab—6 litters, 8 puppies per litter, $400 per puppy*
- *Yellow Lab—6 litters, 8 puppies per litter, $400 per puppy*
- *Subtract one puppy for each Grandkid (5 puppies total) 6 litters x 8 puppies per litter x 2 Labs = 96 total puppies*
  96 total puppies minus 5 puppies for grandkids, minus 12 puppies for Daddy Dog = 79 sold
- *Gross Revenue = $31,675*

<u>Expenses</u>

- *Chocolate Lab $350*
- *Yellow Lab $350*
- *Food @ 25 per month = $300 per year for 10 years = $3,000*
- *Vet bills @ $500 per year (Grandpa will pay anything over $500) = $5,000*
- *Miscellaneous expenses = $900*
- *Total Expenses = $9,600*

Net Revenue: $31,675—$9,600 = $22,075
Amount for Each Grandchild = $4,415

I finished reading the document as we pulled into the driveway of a suburban home about 10 miles from where we'd started. By then, I had no doubt why we were there.

"Let's go," Pat urged as soon as he turned off the ignition.

One would have been hard-pressed to single out this house from the others on the street: all-beige stucco with Spanish tile roofing of burnt-orange color, all a uniform distance from the road, with driveways perpendicular to the street and parallel with one another, and all with perfect lawns and hedges neatly lining the walkway heading to the front door.

Pat approached the front door and rang the bell. I lagged behind, still pondering the Puppy Partner agreement. I assumed that Pat intended to act upon the proposal, and I was pretty certain the action was about to start.

A blonde woman in her late thirties wearing jeans and a t-shirt answered the door.

"You must be Pat."

"Yes, I am," Pat answered, adding rhetorically, "How'd you guess?"

"I'm Melissa," she said, extending her hand and appropriately ignoring Pat's question.

I followed Pat and Melissa into the family room and, at Melissa's request, Pat and I took a seat on the couch. Melissa politely offered us something to drink. We politely declined.

"Well," she sighed as if something horrible was about to happen, "let's get it over with."

She quickly moved to a door that opened out from the family room into the garage and flung it open without hesitation. For a moment, nothing happened as she peered into the darkness of the garage. Then a slightly overweight Yellow Lab with a graying snout eased through the opening and headed slowly in our direction with tags tinkling.

Melissa left the door open as she watched the Lab slowly cross the room. The Lab was in no hurry, stopping to stretch her left hind leg by extending it up and outward, and then continuing on until her nose was touching my knee in anticipation of some petting.

As I reached out to pat the lethargic Lab on the head, a new motion from the garage door caught my eye. I looked up just in time to see a fuzzy little head peek up over the garage step, peering into the family room. Like her mom, it was obvious she'd been unexpectedly roused from her slumber. Nonetheless, she was quicker to wake and was instantly excited that there were new folks in the family room, one of whom was petting her mom.

The tiny bundle of soft golden fur was tall enough to easily get her front legs up onto the steps and well into the room, but still lacked the strength to quickly pull her heavier hind end up and over the final barrier to regain access to her mom. With a bit of a struggle, she managed to get one hind paw up on the step and with herculean effort used the toe-hold to hoist the rest of her pudgy body onto the family-room floor.

As soon as she cleared the step, she bounded directly to me on the sofa, placed both front paws as high as possible on my left shin, and whined while bouncing up and down on her hind legs in a futile effort to jump up onto the couch. Poor mom kept her head in position to be petted, but had no realistic way to compete for my attention. I immediately stopped petting her head and in one fluid motion scooped the eight-week-old pup from the floor and into my arms. Within a matter of seconds, the ball of wiggle had squirmed deep into my lap, found my shiny wedding ring, scratched my hand while eagerly exploring the ring, and yelped loudly when a tiny sharp tooth of hers caught behind the gold band.

The wiggling, scratching, and chewing went largely unnoticed by me. She was absolutely adorable and, as crazy as the grand scheme read on paper, I realized that the Mountain View Puppy Partners was open for business.

Melissa was clearly feeling both relief and loss. The little female Lab, who would become the foundation of Pat's new enterprise with the grandchildren, was the last unsold pup in an original litter of ten. This would be Sunshine's last litter, and Melissa had been contemplating holding onto the last little one to keep Sunshine on her toes and to learn from her well-trained mom before eventually taking on her own maternal role in their canine family. Melissa's husband's new job and imminent relocation put a stop to that plan of succession.

Pat paid for the puppy, all the while assuring Melissa that the female Lab was going to a wonderful home with loving children to help care for her. He thoughtfully spared her the elaborate plan to get another Lab puppy and to breed each dog six times over a ten-year period for a business clearly focused on raising funds for college. Melissa, already in the throes of separation anxiety, didn't seem particularly prepared to deal with that.

I carried the pup to the truck and was entirely smitten as she snuggled into a comfortable position in my arms, then seemed to drift into a sound slumber by the time I tried to gently free my hand to open the truck door. Pat beat me to the door and opened it for me.

As I sat down, careful not to wake the sleeping puppy, he produced the perfect cardboard box from the bed of the old truck and placed it on the floor next to my feet. I eased the pup out of my arms and into the box without waking her. The box contained a hand towel and a small, brand-new chew toy.

"Yep, she's a cutie!" he proclaimed, looking into the box one last time before closing the truck door. We were back on the road and headed to our second stop before we finally found time to discuss the Puppy Partner papers.

"So, you're going into the puppy-raising business?" I asked.

"Well, technically not until the grandkids each raise $15 and officially sign on as partners," he explained.

"So what happens to the new puppy if they don't agree, or can't raise the money?" I asked innocently.

With a wry smile and quick glance in my direction, he noted, "I'm betting that their very smart and industrious parents will help them raise the money and sign the contract. Right?"

I wanted to question the feasibility and assumptions of his business plan, or discuss the extraordinary effort that would be required on his part, and ours. I also wanted to discuss the ramifications of a failed partnership on his future relationship with his grandchildren.

Instead, I simply replied, "Right."

I understood that there was absolutely no chance of altering the plan. It was already in motion, and we were on our way to the next stop, a farm in Livermore with another litter of Labs—this time chocolate ones.

We pulled into a dilapidated old farm littered with broken-down equipment and rusting parts. A crusty old farmer in stereotypical overalls appeared from nowhere and begrudgingly directed us toward an old shed, pointing toward the door.

"You let 'em out, you get 'em back in," he muttered over his shoulder as he headed back to his own work.

We slowly cracked open the door to the 5'x 5' shed and squeezed into the room. As soon as we pulled on the cord, a single overhead bulb cast light on some pretty horrid conditions. Six dark brown balls of fur scrambled over one another and our feet, squeezing between our legs and not bothering to avoid the urine puddles and tiny piles of poop located randomly around the dirt floor. The haggard mom ignored us, choosing to remain tightly curled up in the corner.

The stench of the shed, with its closed door and the six pups scrambling through excrement over one another, then over our feet, was too much to stand for any length of time. The pups were pretty young to be leaving their mom—likely not fully weaned—but it was probably better to take one early than to let it remain in this shed.

Pat reached down and picked up one of the not quite six-week-old pups, holding it with one hand at the scruff of its neck and the other supporting its butt. Four paws and a protruding bare belly faced in my direction. He lifted the pup to my eye level and shoved it toward my face.

"Female?" he inquired.

I looked carefully but couldn't completely make out the anatomy. There was clearly something between the hind legs, but it was so tiny, it could have been swollen female parts, or tiny, under-developed male parts. I was embarrassed, but I honestly couldn't tell. I started to make a guess—female—but considered the consequences of being wrong. My father-in-law would never let me live it down, and we would have to make a second trip to this hell hole.

"Can't tell," I muttered sheepishly.

"What?" Pat asked, clearly displeased with his naïve young son-in-law.

The shed conditions were so unbearable that Pat didn't take the time to probe my gender indecision any further. He handed me the pup, physically manipulating my grasp to mimic his until I was able to extend the pup out, legs first, for his own inspection.

"Girl," he said definitively as soon as he got a quick peek between her legs. "Let's go!"

"You sure? How could you see that so quickly?" I asked.

Pat rolled his eyes, further mocking my lack of experience in such critical and sensitive matters.

I was still regretting my indecisiveness when the door to the shed suddenly flew open and bright sunshine replaced the bulb's dim light. Pat leaned forcefully against me, shoulder on shoulder, until I stumbled out into the farmyard still holding the pup. Pat stepped out behind me and tightly closed the door before the remaining five pups could escape. We both took exaggerated gasps of fresh air.

The little Lab joined us in struggling to adjust to the bright light. It occurred to me that this might be the first time she'd been exposed to full sunlight. She squinted, then lowered her eyelids. She, too, was adorable, but would require a good scrubbing before anyone invited her to cuddle.

Pat had a few choice words for the old farmer and the squalid shed. The farmer waited until Pat finished berating him for the despicable conditions, then asked with heartless calm, "You want the damn dog or not?"

Pat stared at the old man without responding. The man suddenly moved toward me, reaching out firmly, if not aggressively, to take the pup. My arms were extended to keep the odor of the pup at arm's length. I instinctively drew her in close as the man's rough grimy hands neared.

"Wait!" Pat cried. "I'll take her."

Pat pulled out a wad of cash, acknowledging that the old man's advertisement about the pups specifically noted "CASH ONLY." He counted out three hundred dollars and put them into the man's outstretched palm.

The man counted the money and calmly stated, "That'll be $325."

"The ad said $300," Pat said, now furious.

"That was before you insulted me," the farmer replied without emotion.

"That's absurd!" Pat retorted.

The farmer looked Pat directly in the eye, opened the hand clutching the cash, and let each bill float from his palm to the ground.

"Put the damn dog back in the shed, and remember: You let 'em out, you put 'em back!" He turned slowly and began walking back toward his dilapidated house.

"No!" Pat shouted.

The farmer turned around in time to see Pat drop an additional twenty-dollar bill and a five on the pile of cash.

In haste to escape further extortion, we jumped into the truck with the pup and Pat sped away angrily. The box Pat had carefully prepared for the second pup was still in the bed of the truck. I thought about putting her in the same box as the first Lab, who was still sleeping soundly, but was a little concerned about their bonding so soon. I was also concerned about the smell of the chocolate contaminating the yellow, so I decided to hold onto the chocolate.

The chocolate pup, caked with feces and smelling of stale urine, created an unbearable fragrance in the truck's cab. We stood it only until we got to the main road and pulled into a convenience store on the corner. I jumped out quickly, still holding the pup, to avoid vomiting out the truck window.

We were forced to put the new pup into her own box in the back of the truck. Feeling terrible about making her ride outside, we decided to put the box with the first pup back there too. Maybe the presence of one would comfort the other, even though they were in separate boxes.

"It's only a short ride," I rationalized, sensing Pat's concern.

Pat and I made it back to the ranch by 1:00 p.m. Pat was actually right this time. It hadn't taken too awfully long. A couple of quick stops and two puppies later, we were home.

By the time we arrived, the pups were both crying for their moms. Pat decided to give them both flea-baths in preparation for a big night of play and the new joyful life they were about to inherit.

"I can take it from here," he indicated as he ran warm water into the outdoor utility sink. I was anxious to get to my gumbo and writing chores, but was suddenly, irresistibly drawn to the bathing of the tiny little pups.

"I'll help you get started," I offered.

"Fine," he said, handing me the shampoo.

Given her nasty condition, we started with the chocolate. As filthy as she looked, she was so tiny that it took Pat only a few minutes to scrub her up and thoroughly rinse her from head to tail. She sat shivering in the utility sink for the entire ordeal, even though we made every effort to warm the water to an ideal temperature.

When done, Pat handed her to me and reached into the other box for the yellow. I was prepared with a large soft towel and sat out on the front porch of their home, gently rubbing and drying the adorable chocolate pup.

The soft towel was clearly more pleasurable than the warm water, and she responded with wagging tail and tiny tongue kisses on my hands. Smaller and younger than the yellow, the chocolate couldn't have been more precious.

I continued to hug and rub her with the towel well beyond what was necessary to get extraneous water out of her fur. I had a hard time putting her down, anticipating the line of family members who would be vying for her attention later in the evening, realizing this would probably be my only turn.

Finally drawing myself away, I gave her back to Pat and took the opportunity to slip away and do my own chores. As I might have suspected, he'd created the perfect wooden box for the two pups, complete with an old, flowered comforter from the guest bedroom as their bedding. The little chocolate, now smelling like a puppy should, buried herself in the soft fabric.

I found plenty of time to shower and make my gumbo, and even a little time to reluctantly work through editorial comments on my articles. Betty and her mom came home with the kids just in time to clean up, take a ceremonial bite of the leftover applesauce, and prepare for the onslaught of family members.

Pat kept the puppies in the garage and out of sight until the five grandchildren arrived. My part now completed, I joined the rest of the family as Pat orchestrated the launch of the Mountain View Puppy Partnership.

The grandchildren squealed with delight at the discovery

of the two adorable pups in a box in the corner of the garage. Later, Pat sat them all down in the family room, no small task itself, and presented them with their partnership option. The two grandchildren who could read a little, tried. The rest just listened. All wanted to start working immediately to raise their fifteen dollars.

That evening was followed by a decade of elation over each new litter, sadness over pups that didn't make it, and constant communication between the business partners. Pat stayed true to the agreement in caring for the pups and the business, but more importantly kept the grandchildren informed about the status of the pups and the business. His monthly newsletter, "Puppy Partners Update," was religiously created and mailed each month to the grandchildren, who anticipated its arrival and either read, or were read, every word. Pat told stories about the mommy dogs and their pups, gave suggestions about how the grandchildren could best use their money for college, and shared the exact expenditures and revenues associated with the business.

The Puppy Partners ended as planned on October 11, 1997. As Pat had intended, the oldest grandchild was at the time completing applications for Fall 1998 admission to college. None of the skeptical parents had counted on the Puppy Partnership proceeds as a college fund. We were shocked when the final profit arrived.

Pat, the chocolate named "Mocha," and the yellow named "McKenzie," exceeded all expectations. The 103 puppies from 13 litters sold for more than anyone ever anticipated. They also produced adorable lifelong pets for our families. Each grandchild eventually had to leave their pets behind, but they started college with $4,652.34 from the partnership. The joint enterprise gave them all a firm appreciation for what it meant to dream, to plan for those dreams, and to take action to fulfill those dreams.

Caring for 103 puppies over a 10-year period for a planned $4,652 return per grandchild may not seem like the most efficient fund raising strategy; certainly not a sound plan to assure college access. But Pat was unafraid of taking the steps needed to achieve a big, audacious dream.

The grandchildren begged to visit each new litter, all while hanging on every word of the Puppy Partner Update. Each new litter was a new opportunity for Grandpa to reach out to his grandchildren and build a stronger relationship.

If left to my own choices and priorities, I wouldn't have planted the trees, and I certainly wouldn't have gone shopping for puppies, but Pat's unabashed dreaming was contagious.

Not all dreams come true, but none come true unless they can be visualized and shaped into a meaningful plan. Furthermore, none come through unless someone takes action toward fulfilling the plan. Pat's puppy partner dream seemed absurd. It wasn't.

While the puppies grew, so did the Redwoods on the hill. The trees now tower majestically, side-by-side, over the ridge behind Pat and Joanne's ranch. The two largest, Joanne's and Pat's, anchor the cascading silhouette of trees reaching out to either side. Each of the thirteen trees is named after a family member.

Each tree was planted with care and an accompanying ceremony on a day when there were undoubtedly other priorities on the "to-do" list of the planters and onlookers. Each tree represented a dream fulfilled, one planting at a time.

PERSISTENCE

CHAPTER FOUR

As I stand admiring the new benches I've just built, Bo dashes directly behind me. Startled, I twist away and catch a whiff that momentarily convinces me that the skunk has squirted Bo a second time. Soon, I realize the horrid odor is not distinctively skunk. The putrid and unidentifiable smell is a unique combination of malodorous scents, all of which are actually coming from me. The soiled clothes from yesterday's chores, now further contaminated by horse manure and urine, and finished off with a hint of residual skunk juice, is nearly unbearable. I badly need a shower and change of clothes.

As I round the corner of the barn and stride toward the house, Nellie catches my eye from the front pasture, where she is grazing leisurely. The sun is high and the dew on the grass is completely dried, reminding me once again that the day is no longer young. I decide that taking a shower now would take up costly time, and many of the items on my unwritten "to do" list would just get me dirty all over again. Besides, one of the perks of being alone is only needing to worry about offending myself. I read somewhere that the cells in your nose habituate to most bad odors in under ten minutes, which sounds optimistic to me. Nonetheless, I should cherish the most precious things on this special day, and Nellie's on the top of that list.

I approach the four-rail front pasture fence, climbing over it using the rails like a staircase—up one side, over the top, and down the other. I lean back against the fence and watch Nellie closely, jealous of her leisurely life. She's grazing about seventy-five yards away and showing no sign of noticing or acknowledging my presence in her pasture.

"Nell," I call, slightly raising my voice to ensure that she hears me, but with the same intonation I've used since before she was weaned. If she's learned anything, it's to come when I call. I'm not surprised that she doesn't immediately look up in response to the sound of her name. Observing her almost every day since she was born just over two years ago, I've learned that she likes to play "hard to get." Finally, she nonchalantly looks in my direction, still grinding grass with her back teeth. Then, without hesitation or looking away, she begins slowly moving in my direction. Her pace gradually quickens, first to a trot and within several strides into a full gallop.

Stand your ground, I remind myself.

She continues to gain speed, quickly closing the gap between us. I'm relatively certain of her final intentions, but if I'm wrong, the rest of my day will end up even worse than it started.

I move forward two steps away from the fence and further into the pasture, plant my boots shoulder-width apart, and stand tall. The ground shakes as twelve-hundred pounds of chestnut-and-white horse thunder in my direction with nostrils flaring and blonde mane flowing. Two other horses in the pasture slowly raise their heads, mildly interested.

My heart rate rises ever so slightly as I slowly raise my right hand, palm opened toward the barreling mass, and extend it in front of my chest with elbow slightly bent. My hand shakes slightly despite my 99 percent confidence that I know how this will end.

Five yards out, Nellie suddenly extends both front legs, driving her hooves into the badly worn grass and dry summer dirt of her pasture. Her blonde tail, which matches her mane, tucks suddenly. She lowers her hind quarters and simultaneously locks her back legs in a forward position paralleling the front, lightly dragging herself across the ground. Her hooves slide through the soft dirt and thin grass, leaving four small parallel trenches.

I'm a fraction of a second away from falling back toward the fence when her slide abates and she settles to a stop. The pink nose at the end of the white stripe running the length of her face is resting softly against the palm of my hand.

"Whoaaaa, Nellie," I say softly, well after the command has any value. It's the familiar phrase for which she's named.

Nellie and I have played this game since I put her in one pasture and the mare who foaled her in another; she was four months old. Having been directly involved with the artificial insemination of that mare, having watched her extraordinary birth, and having been with her ever since, I have a very strong bond of trust with Nellie. But she's more than half a ton of bone and muscle, and still has the questionable body control of a lanky two-year-old filly.

I stand in the field rubbing Nellie's striped forehead with my fingertips. Her nostrils flair with each exhale as she tries to catch her breath. My instincts tell me that today is the day, but I still don't want to pressure either of us with a firm commitment or deadline.

Besides, I've clearly forbidden myself from setting specific accomplishable goals for my day alone on the farm. I've already suffered one setback after another, and establishing any more definite, structured objectives would further detract from the gift of being able to choose whatever meaningless activity I want.

Who could've imagined the stinking, gorging, pile of crap this day was becoming? It could all be salvaged with one spontaneous act, an act which I have been anxiously anticipating, but for which I will never be fully prepared.

Nellie tires of my direct attention and begins to further thin the grass around my feet.

"How about today?" I ask calmly.

Indifferent, Nellie continues grazing with no indication that she understands or cares. However, when I walk away, her indifference fades and she follows me like a small child as I walk along the fence line to the gate on which her halter and lead line hang.

Nellie's halter slips easily over her nose, then up and over her forehead and ears. She shakes her head in gentle protest until I recognize that one ear is bent forward and trapped under the halter. As soon as I release her ear, she's content.

I lead her to the barn, and once again marvel at the control that the thin nylon halter provides me over the huge two-year-old horse. Horses must follow their noses, and altering the position of a horse's nose turns out to be a very easy thing to accomplish with the simple use of a working halter.

Nellie still has a lot to learn. She leads well, stands for the farrier to trim her hooves, is patient in cross-ties when being groomed, is comfortable around electric clippers, and will allow you to put a number of things on her back, including a blanket and saddle. But this list does not include people. No one has ever been on Nellie's back.

As the cowboys say, "She ain't broke to ride."

Eugene was broken to ride by a professional cowboy, albeit a very impatient one. He was rough on Eugene, and Eugene returned the favor. Betty and I watched in agony as the two fought it out over three full days. Our only satisfaction was in seeing the cowboy spend more time in the dirt than he did on Eugene. Just like in the westerns.

Eugene eventually gave in to the cowboy's rough demands, but not without an impressive fight. Many years later, he still likes to fight aggressive demands from highly qualified riders, offering up strong resistance to every command.

Ironically, he's a "helper" to those who mount him with no preconceived notion of what he should do, or how they might get him to do it. He works hard to interpret the unclear signals of children, of the timid, and of novice riders. He only takes advantage of those who try to take advantage of him, and Betty is just fine with that.

Seeing the effect of old-fashioned horse-breaking on Eugene's psyche and the way he still responds, or doesn't, to authority, I decide to try a different approach with Nellie—a kinder, gentler approach. Dozens of books, videos, and internet sites describe how to break horses without excessive force. I read and watched them all, and Nellie and I have completed all of the necessary groundwork.

This work includes desensitizing the young horse, who's naturally afraid of every strange sound and movement. Teaching a young horse to move away from pressure, to accept and respond to a bit and bridle, and to be comfortable wearing a blanket and saddle are the basics. Nellie was an eager and quick learner. We've spent the last two months mastering each stage in every book and resource.

Regardless of how much you put into this groundwork, sooner or later someone has to choose a specific day, mount the horse for the very first time, and see what happens. From the day Nellie was born, I was determined to be that someone. Standing with Nellie in her pasture, I decided this would be that day.

I will ride Nellie for the first time on Father's Day. It's a very unique and personal present that she will unknowingly, and perhaps unwillingly, give me.

Nellie senses something's up and is a little agitated when I cinch her saddle slightly tighter than ever before and eventually insert the bit and bridle. We've completed this exercise dozens of times for practice, but she somehow knows that this might not end with me walking her a few laps around the arena and then taking the uncomfortable contraption off of her back. Her ears pin back and she scrapes the ground with her front hoof a few times in mild resistance. Eventually, she begrudgingly stands quietly.

In the arena, I take a moment to admire her standing tall, wearing her new leather saddle with matching reins. I'd love to take a picture with my mobile phone, but as I reach for it in my pocket, I remember that the battery died earlier in the morning while I was dealing with the manure spreader.

It's clear that Nellie's nervous, and I begin to question whether this is really the right day. Once I decide to mount her, I have to follow through. If she gets rowdy and tries to buck me off, I'm going to have to stay the course. I can't let her believe she'll decide whether or not she's going to be ridden.

Will I end up having to physically force the issue? Is it even possible to force the issue? I'm not the world's greatest rider and begin to wonder how long I can possibly stay on if she decides to rear and buck. I picture the tough cowboy who broke Eugene, rising from the dusty arena floor and remounting, only to be tossed back into the dirt. More than anything, I wonder how such a contest of wills might affect the trusting relationship Nell and I have developed since her birth.

I've read that easing into the saddle with the slowest distribution of weight on the horse's back is the least intrusive strategy and is most likely to keep the horse calm. This requires placing a heavy, plastic, three-step mounting stool directly beside Nellie, climbing to the top step, and slowly sliding a leg over her back before gently placing my weight onto the saddle.

Nellie stands quietly as I put down the stool, but turns her head and neck around to get a better look at the steps. I pat her neck and gently run my fingers through her mane to reassure her. Her curiosity quickly fades in response to my reassuring words. As I rise to the first step of the perfectly positioned stool, Nellie takes three quick and purposeful side-steps away with her hind legs.

I step down, reposition the stool, and try again. Again, she moves away as soon as I'm up on the first step. The third time I reposition the stool, she doesn't move away until I reach the second step. After about fifteen minutes of this progressive desensitization strategy, I can stand on the third step perfectly positioned at her side.

At this point, the book instructs: "Slowly raise your leg and extend it over the horse's back until your knee is resting on the center of the saddle with only the weight of your leg. Your other leg should remain on the top step of the mounting stool and bear the bulk of your weight."

Nellie stands perfectly still as I raise my right leg and start to extend it out over her back. She continues to stand quietly as I lower my knee into the center of the saddle. Just as I am beginning to feel confident and shift the weight of my leg, she takes another three quick side steps away from the stool. I'm not prepared for this shift, and the sudden lack of support for my right leg causes me to lose my balance. I fall off of the mounting stool and onto the soft arena sand. I probably can't officially count this as being thrown, but I'm dusting myself off and preparing to remount like any good cowboy.

I reposition the stool and try again, assuming that it won't be the last time I'm in the dirt. It isn't.

I chase Nellie around with the stool for nearly half an hour and begin to grow frustrated. Nellie, on the other hand, is calmer and more confident than when we began. I decide to forget the book and move to Plan B. Plan B is more direct, but isn't recommended by the horse book authors.

I slip my left toe into the saddle stirrup with my right leg still firmly planted on the top stair of the stool. As I slowly shift weight onto my left leg in the stirrup, Nellie decides to sidestep one more time. I'm suddenly tired of this game and in one quick motion swing my right leg across Nellie's back and plop my full 220 pounds down into the saddle before she can move away.

Every muscle in my body tenses as I quickly gather the reins, expecting the worst. Nellie immediately extends her front feet about six inches forward and plants them firmly in the sand while simultaneously extending her hind legs backward, bracing them in the same manner.

Without hesitation or my prompting with the reins, she turns her head slowly, then looks up over her left shoulder—directly into my eyes. Her incredulous stare remains constant.

Horses express their emotions with their ears, not their eyes like people and dogs. Ears back mean she's mad, ears forward that she's listening intently, and ears twitching that she's engaged, curious, or just in a playful mood. It's harder to read a horse's eyes, but on this occasion, I can read her piercing stare.

"Really?" she seems to be saying. I notice her ears are moving back toward her neck. "Do you really think I'm going to carry your big ass around this arena?" I can almost hear her thoughts.

Her ears pinned flat against the back of her head continue to express her anger and I wonder if her next move will be to bite my knee, which is clearly within striking distance, less than eight inches from her mouth when she gazes back at me. I pull gently on the right rein to turn her head back forward. She resists. She's not finished staring me down, convincing me she's not going to move a muscle as long as I'm planted on her back.

Eventually, she gives in to the pressure from the bit, slowly straightens her head, and stares forward into the side of the barn. Her legs remain locked like tree trunks.

Our groundwork has included learning the two most important equine commands—"go" and "whoa." The process involved me following her from behind, issuing voice commands and making accompanying motions with long reins to signal starting and stopping. She's learned to move forward on a clucking sound combined with the gentle tap of very loose reins against the side of her neck. Typically, she's quite sensitive and responsive to these cues, at least when I follow her on the ground.

I think carefully about how well she responds to the other command, "whoa," before deciding to try to get her moving. Given that I named her for the express purpose of being able to say "Whoa, Nellie," she's very familiar with the term and will stop on a dime when I use it. At least, she does when I'm standing behind her, pulling back on long reins. Her unfamiliar expression of displeasure gives me pause, but I've gotten this far and might as well keep going.

I place my tongue against the roof of my mouth and pull it down sharply with mouth slightly open. "Cluck." Nothing happens. I do it again in rapid succession and a little louder, "Cluck, cluck." Still no action.

Patient me repeats the sound even louder and taps the reins lightly against the side of her neck. Nothing. One more time, louder, with more reins. Still nothing!

Finally, as instructed by the book, I gently squeeze the inside of my thighs against her belly. More nothing. She doesn't move a muscle and continues to stare forward. Tighter squeeze? To no avail. At this point, one might confuse her with the life-size metal statues that mark the entrances to fancy farms.

I'm a bit perturbed that she's not responding to the commands we've worked so hard to learn. On the other hand, I have no intention of strapping on a pair of spurs and, cowboy-style, whacking her flank.

I spread my legs a bit and bring them back in with a tap on the side of her belly. Nothing. Again and again I try, increasing the intensity each time. Each time I'm fully prepared for the start of the bucking bronco show. No such show.

Stumped, I change tactics completely and decide to sit quietly. Maybe she'll get bored and begin to wander the arena looking for a loose blade of hay. Fifteen minutes later, with Nellie still staring at the side wall of the arena, I abandon this strategy.

I try hard to remember any tips from the stack of horse training books I've read. If she wins by refusing to move the very first time I mount her, I may never get her to move with me in the saddle.

I try to picture actions that have moved her in the past. When she was a foal, she was afraid of everything, and the slightest unexpected motion could send her into a full gallop. Ironically, we've spent two years getting her used to such startling actions. At least that part of the training has worked.

I finally remember the one place on her body that's still a little sensitive to the touch. High on her hind quarter, where her leg connects to her midsection, is a sliver of connective tissue covered with soft, fine fur. Even a gentle rub in that area still elicits a tense reaction and often a stomp of the foot.

My left heel will naturally come very close to this spot if I push the stirrup back forcefully toward her hind leg and turn my heel inward. In my zealous effort to get my heel and the restraining stirrup back far enough, I make contact with the desired area sooner, more squarely, and more forcefully than I intended.

Without warning, Nellie immediately tucks her hind legs underneath her and collapses her rear end to the ground with an audible thud. Her front legs remain locked.

She's gonna roll, I instantly think. She regularly lies down and rolls in the arena to brush flies from her back, Why not do the same to me? I've watched her enough to recognize that, when she lies down, the hind end hits the ground first. Having my leg trapped under a 1200-pound animal is not in any of my plans for the day, so I decide to bail.

I reason that the most likely way to get trapped under the roll is to dismount traditionally from the side, so I lean completely forward in the saddle, lift my lower torso over its back edge, and stretch my legs backward, intending to slide down her back and over her rear. With her front legs still locked, it's simply a matter of using the angle of her back to slip safely to the ground.

Just as my thighs begin to slide across her big hind end, she thrusts upward with her powerful back legs, thrusting her ass high in the air and straightening her hind legs with a forceful buck I never dreamed she could muster. I instinctively reach forward and am barely able to grab the saddle horn with both hands.

By the time I have a firm grasp, my legs are hurtling upward with enough force to carry my torso into the air as well. My death grasp on the saddle horn provides a fixed pivot point and prompts a full back-flip that would be the envy of an Olympic vaulter. Nellie calculates the angle of my descent and carefully lowers her head and shoulders, moving them to the side to provide clearance.

My eyes are still closed and I'm gasping to regain the air forced from my lungs when my back hit hard and flush on the arena floor. I feel a tickle on my face. Is a barn fly really taking the opportunity to walk across my cheek while I'm this vulnerable?

My lungs begin to refill with precious oxygen and the heaving of my chest subsides. I slowly open my eyes to a fuzzy, pink-fleshed muzzle not an inch from the side of my face. The long wispy hairs on Nellie's nose are creating the tickling sensation on my cheek. Either to add insult to injury or to remove arena dirt from my face, she forcefully blows air from her protruding lips, creating a flapping sound and a gentle spray of saliva that is her trademark sign of relaxation.

Her loving nuzzle, which uses the fine hairs that grow long and sporadic around her snout, tempts me to call it a day. Nellie would so love to join the mares back in the field, and I'm not sure I'll make it off the arena floor. I feel completely spent just from the tension of waiting atop her for so long, anticipating a reaction that finally transpired, and never mind everything else I've had to deal with today.

Idiot! I think to myself, still looking up into her curious brown eyes. *What made you believe you could learn to break a horse from reading a book?* I allow myself a moment of self-doubt while I ponder what to do next.

New resolve replaces doubt as my breathing normalizes and Nellie continues to loom over me in a position that feels increasingly smug and dominating. I quickly reach out with an open hand and pop Nellie sharply on the same nose that just lovingly nuzzled me. She jerks her head high into the air and jumps back, startled.

I scramble to my feet in the space she abandons, trying to ignore the dull pain in my back. She continues to back away. I simultaneously grab the reins hanging from her bridle in my right hand and stomp my boots into the ground, moving briskly toward her. Her retreat quickens.

I shake the reins back and forth aggressively, continuing to march toward her retreating chest. I wave my left hand back and forth in front of her face at eye level to heighten the effect. Her legs and hooves are moving furiously in reverse while I continue to invade her space and shake the loose end of the reins in her face.

Horses escape adversity by running forward. Like big delivery trucks, they don't back up well. Unlike big trucks, they have no rearview mirrors. Backing up goes against their basic nature and is a very effective way to punish them. At least that's what the books say.

Her move to dislodge me from the saddle had been artful and effective, but it was a clear act of rebellion. Her training won't progress if she learns that such theatrics will get her out of having to carry me up a steep winding trail on a Sunday ride. The rocks on the trail will feel much worse than the sandy arena.

About halfway through a backwards lap around the arena, Nellie decides she's had enough. She suddenly stops and rears up, striking out towards me with her front hooves. I'm not fully prepared for this second act of rebellion, but instinctively add my free hand to the reins and yank down hard. She immediately settles on all four hooves and reluctantly resumes her retreat. I march toward her with even greater resolve, now thrashing her chest with the loose ends of the reins. So much for the kinder, gentler approach to horse training.

Nellie settles again into retreat. By the time we complete two full backward laps, we're moving in somewhat of a synchronized rhythm.

I stop suddenly, reposition the reins over her head, and without thought or warning place my left boot in the left stirrup. Then, in one motion, I pull myself up and over into the saddle. Nellie is still reeling from the backward motion and stands statue-still while I find the opposite-side stirrup with my right toe.

I cluck once and gently squeeze both legs. She moves forward calmly and instantly. I respond immediately, releasing the pressure on her sides. Just before she approaches the indoor arena wall, I lay the reins gently against the left side of her neck and put gentle pressure on her side with my left leg. She complies and turns sharply to her right. One ear is locked forward—she's listening. The other twitches slightly at full attention—she's anticipating my next command.

"Whoa!" I shout forcefully and without warning. I promptly tighten both reins so that the bit pulls taut against the soft corners of her mouth. I simultaneously lean my head and torso back toward her rear, pushing the stirrups forward and straightening my body like a board. All four of her legs stop moving instantly and she stands quietly, without so much as a tail switch. Immediately, I dismount in one fluid movement. The saddle and bridle are unceremoniously removed. Within minutes, Nellie's back out in the field grazing with Star and Prissy.

Round two obviously went much better than round one and was stopped abruptly to purposely end on a positive note. As much as she needed to be corrected for misbehaving, she needed to be quickly rewarded for compliance. Nothing is more rewarding for Nellie than to be back out in the pasture with her pals.

I have big plans for Nellie. She has a lot to learn in a relatively short time. She needs to go on long trail rides with me, Betty, and Eugene. She has to learn to pull a cart in preparation for giving rides to grandchildren, and when they are old enough, she needs to handle them with care on rides of their own. She has a long way to go.

As I walk toward the house, the pain in my lower back reminds me of my unintended back flip over Nellie's head. The fright and frustration of that moment fade as I picture Nellie's precise turns on command. I'm proud of her recovery from an abysmal start, and equally proud of myself for getting back in the saddle.

Thursday, August 16, 1979

The now familiar sound of gravel startled me once again. Suddenly wide awake and aware that I'd drifted off the edge of Highway 65, I avoided jerking the wheel, slowed down a bit, and eased back onto the road.

"Maybe this is how it's supposed to end," I said, but not

loud enough to hear myself over Donna Summers belting out "Bad Girls" over the radio in my silver 1976 Cutlass Supreme.

Alone in the car at 4:30 a.m., I was headed south. As an early riser who'd had a very long four days, I found it almost impossible to keep my eyes open. I'd have to stop again for coffee, as I had every 50 to 70 miles for the last 200. I'd stopped that often not only to stay awake, but to relieve myself of the coffee from the previous stops. The usual ten-hour drive was turning into thirteen, though that didn't matter at the back end—no one was expecting me.

During the first few hours of the southward, 600-mile trek from Evanston, Illinois to Knoxville, Tennessee, there was no chance of dozing. With the sun fading west in the late summer afternoon, I mentally played and replayed the events of the last few days, then the last few months, then the last few days again, a recurring loop of inquiry into how the totally unexpected had unfolded.

I'd worked hard over the spring and summer trying to finish my master's thesis at The University of Tennessee. My flattering and somewhat surprising acceptance into the rigorous doctoral program in developmental psychology at Northwestern University in Evanston wasn't necessarily contingent upon a finished master's thesis, but I knew that if I left Knoxville before it was complete, the thesis would likely never be finished. Mal, my psych professor and advisor, had convinced me of this, using war story after war story of past students who moved away with the best intentions and never found the proper motivation or support to type the thesis' last word.

On a southern campus, spring and summer were not the two most conducive seasons to discipline oneself to write. Distractions were particularly challenging for a poor graduate student moonlighting as a bartender in the local student pub. I'd spend my days collecting data and working on my thesis, and my nights drawing mugs of draft beer for undergrads. The legal beer drinking age was eighteen then, and the giggling young coeds were out in force every night.

By the time the bar closed, I'd convince myself that I had worked hard enough to justify a few beers of my own and was fortunate enough on occasion to find a pretty Southern coed to join me. Mornings came early, but twenty-three-year-olds found ways to persevere until there was a better occasion to sleep.

In the end, my thesis couldn't compete with Nashville's exciting nightlife. Besides, the data from my thesis would be better utilized in the future, reviewed by my professorial peers in a respectable journal, than it would be on the library shelf. This awareness made it easy to draw beers for potential girlfriends instead of writing up results and discussion sections. My emerging reputation in the field had already been acknowledged by acceptance into a top graduate program. Who needed a master's when you were on the fast track to a doctorate?

I'd never dreamed of getting this far in school. High school was about making grades just good enough to get an athletic scholarship and fulfill a lifelong dream of playing college football. When chronic knee injuries cut short what was an already uninspiring run at NCAA football, I decided to go to graduate school. The plan was to cruise through my undergraduate program at North Carolina University, earning grades just good enough for entry into a program whose reputation would lead to some form of employment in counseling or psychological work with children and youth.

Mal Rosen was an associate professor in the psychology department. A girl I dated during the fall of my senior year took his introductory course on developmental psychology and was inspired by his passionate lectures about children. Knowing my eventual career aspirations, she arranged for me to meet Mal just before the winter break.

The department secretary pointed me down the hall to a nondescript faculty office, where I found a thin man no taller than five-foot-five standing behind a desk littered with manuscripts. He held his glasses' earpiece in one hand, idly spinning the frames around and around. A stapled manuscript was in the other hand, folded back to the reference section. Neither the glasses nor the manuscript held his attention as he gazed toward the ceiling. He appeared to have intentionally removed his glasses to allow a more thoughtful reflection about the accuracy of the reference list.

The floor to ceiling bookshelves behind his desk were overflowing with stacked books and journal volumes. As I approached his desk, he extended the hand holding the glasses, not toward me, but back toward the bookshelf.

"Have you read these books?" he inquired in what seemed

a merely rhetorical tone.

He was standing in front of the shelves, preventing a full view. Nonetheless, his slight frame obstructed only a few volumes from my field of vision. I studied the books I could see and was prepared to confess to a blanket "no," when I finally recognized a title on the bottom shelf—*The Roots of Sharing, Caring, and Helping* by Mussen and Eisenberg-Berg. I only remembered it because of the coauthor's double "berged" name.

"I've read that one," I said, pointing to the book I'd just finished reading as an assignment in my social development class. The book had intrigued me, and I was surprised to see it on the shelf. I would become even more puzzled as I got to know Mal and his egocentric tendencies.

"I've read them all," he said, matter-of-factly putting his glasses back on and returning to the manuscript's reference section.

"Wow," I said, trying to quickly estimate how many books were on those shelves.

"So, I see you got an A in Stats from Dr. Leyman," he said nonchalantly.

I couldn't decide if I should be impressed or distressed. I didn't expect him to know my name, much less my grade in a specific course. On his cluttered desk, my transcript was nowhere in view.

"Your friend Ms. James says you want to work with children," not allowing time for a reply to the statement about my grades.

"Yes, I do," I responded.

"Are you any good?" he asked.

"I think so," I muttered.

"Well, I'm damn good!" he proclaimed, strengthening my growing impression that he was the cockiest little guy I'd ever encountered.

I stood in front of his desk in silence while he continued to review the reference list. Finally, he bent down behind the desk and picked up a cardboard box, eighteen inches long, seven inches wide, and three inches deep. I recognized its contents immediately.

Handing me the box along with a single sheet of paper containing scribbled handwritten notes, he asked, "How long will it take you?"

I took the uncovered box without even glancing at its contents and began to review the notes on the paper. "I can have it in the morning," I said with quickly growing confidence.

"Good," he mumbled, once again examining the reference list. Arrogant little twit was probably looking to make certain the author had appropriately cited Mal's own journal articles before passing judgment on the worth of the manuscript, I thought.

"I'll be in at 8:30," he added without looking up.

The familiar box contained a neatly stacked deck of computer punch cards, the kind used to do statistical analysis on mainframe computers. Personal computers would render their use archaic in a few short years. Until then, the state-of-the-art process of running statistics on a mainframe computer was more efficient and accurate than paper and pencil calculations, but still cumbersome and overly mechanical.

The punch cards contained data generated by a college student sitting in front of an IBM 029 keypunch machine resembling a grossly oversized electric typewriter with an expanded keyboard. Each character stroke on the keyboard produced a small hole in an originally blank 3x7 card. Each card eventually contained up to 80 character strokes and, when ejected from the machine on command, added to the emerging stack of data for a specific research project.

In the social sciences, each card represented a subject. In Mal's studies, the subjects were children. The box contained data on over 750 children in one of Mal's studies.

Creating the "data deck" was a tedious job for academically struggling freshmen and sophomores. Some could sit in front of the keypunch for hours, acquiring extra credit for the sole purpose of eking out a passing grade in their introductory psychology course. Creating the much smaller complementary stack of cards in the FORTRAN computer language, which would inform the mainframe computer how to read and analyze the data, was a more skilled task and one most often learned in the first few years of graduate school.

During our junior year, my roommate, a computer science major, needed data entry and programming help on a required class project. Over a few intensive days of helping him meet a deadline, I learned the basics of FORTRAN.

Mal's handwritten notes outlined some relatively simple descriptive statistics and t-tests to be developed from the box of data. Six or seven punched cards would contain enough commands to tell the mainframe exactly what was needed.

The only tricky part of Mal's job was getting the data in the queue for mainframe processing in time for the job to be run overnight and the results picked up by dawn. Desktop computing, not to mention e-mail, existed only in the dreams of the most progressive electrical engineers at the time.

My roommate and I managed to create the control cards and submit them, with the data deck, at the university's mainframe computing building with a few minutes to spare. The job ran flawlessly, so I had the results in hand for Mal when he arrived at his office at 8:20 the next morning.

"Looks good," he said nonchalantly as he flipped through the pages of computer output.

Suddenly, with much more passion and focus, he said, "I want to introduce you to my daughter, Lisa." The precocious three-year-old at his side took a large step forward and eagerly extended her hand like a miniature real estate broker at an open house.

"I'm Lisa and I'm almost FOUR!" she said, glaring at her father for misrepresenting her true age. Through nature or nurture, she had already acquired Mal's confidence.

"Hi, I'm Adam," I said, looking down into excited blue eyes.

"Here's an idea," Mal told Lisa, squatting to be at eye level with the preschooler. "Why don't you take Adam over to the center and introduce him to your teachers?"

"Sure," she responded, reaching up with her tiny hand. I extended the pointer finger on my left hand and she wrapped her soft little fingers around it.

"Adam may want to work with me at the center. What do you think?"

"Great," she replied, leading me out of the office.

Henderson House was the on-campus preschool that Lisa attended and Mal operated as a child development laboratory. I passed it daily on my way to classes, routinely observing the joyful children on the playground.

I met Lisa's teachers that morning. Later that day, at Mal's suggestion, I agreed to work there on his research projects until I finished my undergraduate program.

It was the start of a lifelong relationship with Mal as both mentor and colleague, a very productive, though seemingly unlikely, partnership. We were mirror opposites in size, personality, and style. He was tiny. I was large. He preferred to be alone. I wanted as many people around as possible. He liked control. I didn't mind being told what to do. He had big ideas grounded in elaborate but sound theories. I could get stuff done.

Somehow our complementary styles clicked, and we quickly went on a roll, carving out quite a reputation in research on children's friendships and peer relations. We had one paper accepted for publication before we left North Carolina, and three more were in press by the second year of my master's program.

Just before graduation, Mal took a similar job at the University of Tennessee and asked me to transfer there to stay with him.

"Sure," I responded as nonchalantly as Lisa had once agreed to accompany me across campus.

Two years later, the Cutlass was taking me back to Tennessee under entirely different circumstances.

My success in academia was derived from Mal's "big picture" tutelage combined with his unwavering encouragement of independence and risk-taking. No idea was too big, or too silly, to pursue. In retrospect, we had plenty of big and silly ideas, but Mal created the safe space for necessary trial and error. The reaction to error determines the willingness to undertake future trials, and the willingness to digest the failure and keep trying is, I discovered, of paramount importance.

One success out of 20 attempts yields a low batting average in baseball. In science and social science, one major finding per 20 or more attempts can lead to a Nobel Prize.

Mal's swagger was also a bit contagious. At age 23, with a pocket full of well-regarded publications on my résumé, I'd been recruited to, and been accepted at, Northwestern University, a first-tier doctoral program. Brimming with confidence, I excitedly left Tennessee for Evanston, Illinois, which is just outside of Chicago.

No sooner was I in town than I panicked. I was suddenly sure that I would never measure up; I knew that every doctoral student at Northwestern had at least a pocketful of publications, and I convinced myself that all of them had read all of the books on Mal's bookshelves, too. Many were older—over 30. Two were even 35! Some had children of their own to study. Not one moonlighted as a bartender.

The confidence Mal had instilled in me over the past two years evaporated in the first full meeting between incoming Ph.D. students and faculty members. During the initial introductions, students were asked to tell the group, including the faculty, about their most recent research. The first three students mentioned paper after paper, all published in much more prestigious journals than mine, and quickly and eloquently summarized their major findings.

As my turn rolled around, I unexpectedly lapsed into a full-blown panic attack. I couldn't get out my name and previous institutions without pausing for a deep breath. I was convinced they could all see my heart beating through my preppy, button-downed blue shirt and hear every hesitation in my cracking voice. My pen rattled on the desk as I dropped it to place my now shaking hands in my lap, lest they think I was having a seizure. At this point, it might actually have been advantageous to feign a grand mal.

"I'm . . . Adam . . . from North Carolina . . . and, and . . . Tennessee. I, uh, have a couple of papers . . ." *Breathe, breathe—try to breathe.* "But my major professor wrote most of the narrative," I was finally able to utter. I quickly followed with a sweeping hand gesture to signal the person sitting next to me that I was done.

I was mortified. Over the next 88 minutes, I either stared

at my watch or the single sheet of paper on the desk listing the faculty. As soon as the chair of the department adjourned the meeting, I slunk along the side wall, studying only my shoes, eager to escape onto the open campus, where I could find anonymity.

That evening I decided to try to forget about my professional future and carve out a new personal life in Evanston. I asked around for the most popular hangout for new graduate students, thinking the directions I received were to a bar. Eager to get out, I showed up at the suggested spot around 8:00 p.m. It turned out to be a small café in the recreation room of a graduate student housing complex.

Granted, there were a nice number of grad students in the room, eating and studying, or doing homework. Many were there with their own children. The only entertainment was an intense game of chess in the corner between two students from India, who obviously were in the midst of a series of matches. I was well received by the students, but it wasn't exactly what I was looking for on my first night out in town.

I eventually found my way to the undergraduate section of Evanston and stood on the most central corner I could find with the greatest field of vision for surveying pedestrian traffic. The streets were active, and I watched for groups of three or more late teens and twenty-somethings moving in and out of specific bars and restaurants.

Bartending had taught me that "group" bars are easier to infiltrate than "couples" bars and not as depressing as "individual" bars filled with lonely folks drowning their sorrows. In very little time, I honed in on a corner bar attracting group after group of lively undergraduates.

Upon entering this bar on this night, though, I immediately discovered that a stranger walking solo into a "group" bar doesn't feel the same way about it as a group-member, or better yet, a recognizable bartender.

This bar was hopping with activity. Rowdy undergrads shouted and cheered as others chugged beer from pitchers. Suddenly, this was as unappealing as the chess match in the dorm rec room.

Rather than finding new friends, I quickly settled next to a lonely guy at the bar and used liquor to ease my professional distress. In retrospect, it would have felt much more appropriate had I done the same in an "individual" bar. I was as miserable as any twit sitting alone on any stool in any vibrant college town.

The situation didn't improve over the next eight days. I kept my head down through a series of orientation sessions and somehow managed to avoid another panic attack. My pre-furnished apartment became my only solace, and I stayed in bed watching reruns of "The Andy Griffith Show" and Atlanta Braves late-season baseball whenever possible.

On my tenth day in Evanston, there was another required meeting between the faculty and the new doctoral students. I was petrified that I'd be called upon to speak. Recurring panic attacks had never been an issue for me, but the thought of another one out of the blue clearly created a self-fulfilling prophecy.

The meeting began without my involvement and I was getting more comfortable with my anonymity in the back of the room when the department chair announced that most faculty members had selected whom they'd be advising. "Most" was the operative word. He proceeded to name 13 of the 15 new graduate students, along with the professors who'd selected them. When he was done, my name had not been called. The only other uncalled name was that of Ming Lee from China, who spoke very little English despite questionably high scores on her language exams. Ming hung her head, clearly understanding what had just been communicated.

"Adam and Ming, we are still exploring options for you!" the chair said without explanation or overt empathy.

The meeting ended immediately and quite awkwardly, with faculty scurrying out and avoiding eye contact. No one had the slightest interest in working with or advising me!

I returned to my apartment, threw some clothes into a suitcase, and headed south. I didn't cry until I hit the Indiana border, then didn't stop crying until crossing back into Tennessee.

Frequent, soul-searching pit-stops stretched the entire trip back to Knoxville. I arrived back on the UT campus just before 2:00 a.m. Still in possession of the key to our academic building, I entered through the back loading-dock door and went straight to the graduate student lounge. A familiar sofa was waiting in the otherwise deserted building. I plopped onto the couch and slept until the morning staff opened the building to the public at 7:50 a.m.

Except for the few items in my bag, all my possessions were in Illinois, and I was back in Tennessee without plans or a place to go. The student lounge was as good a spot as any for a guy without an apartment in town, and whose local friends he'd said goodbye to a couple of weeks back.

Besides, I wanted to see Mal as soon as he arrived at work. I wasn't looking forward to the exchange, but knew I needed to explain before he heard an embellished account of my disappearance from concerned colleagues at Northwestern.

I was splashing my face at the sink in the second floor bathroom down the hall from Mal's office, still deciding how to describe the fiasco, when he entered the bathroom directly behind me. Through the reflection in the mirror, I could see his expressionless eyes for a moment. I dried my face with a paper towel, buying time to construct an explanation.

"Guess you weren't planning on seeing me here, were you?" was all I could utter.

"Not really," he said, continuing to mask any emotion as he moved in front of the urinal on the opposite wall.

I continued to dab myself with the paper towel and tucked the tails of my wrinkled shirt into my khakis without comment. Then I was back in front of the mirror, feigning a search of my nose for a non-existent zit, when he approached the adjacent sink to wash his hands.

"Not the right time, eh?"

I pondered whether he was suggesting that it wasn't the right time to talk, the right time for me to be at Northwestern, or the right time to find a zit on my nose.

"Guess not" was my safe reply to all three.

"I wondered," he added and walked through the bathroom door and down the hall toward his office. I instinctively followed, stopping short of entering his office.

Another wave of shame pushed my slumping shoulders even further toward the ground as I tried to convince my brown Top-Siders to take the final few steps into Mal's office. I'd travelled all night across four states, through wave after wave of agonizing doubt and self-reproach, dreading this moment, but knowing no other option.

He—no, we—had worked so hard to get me accepted into a premier program. I had blown it and was back in Knoxville with my tail between my legs in under two weeks.

"Rest up and see if you can have these done in a couple of days."

Mal was suddenly in front of me, outside of his office, thrusting another box of computer cards in my direction. I was furious. Wasn't he going to ask me about Evanston? Wasn't he disappointed? Was he sadistically pleased that I ran back to Tennessee and showed up at his office first? I hadn't even told my family.

"Sure," I muttered, grabbing the box from his hand. Turning toward the stairwell, I tried not to stomp my feet like the antisocial preschoolers we'd studied.

Before sleeping for a full three days, I took the card deck directly to the computer center and finished the analysis for Mal. He never thanked me, just kept giving me more computer analyses to do. Mal had yet to fill my position as a research assistant, and because I hadn't turned in my master's thesis, I was eligible to slide right back into the position as a continuing graduate student. My job at the bar was still open as well. Within a few days, I had slipped back into my old lifestyle of academia during the day and age-appropriate revelry at night.

The bartending gig included short-order grill responsibilities during the lunch hour. The tavern was well-known in this part of the college town for a great burger and curly fries, and regularly ran a Friday special. Shortly after my return to town, Mal and one of my other favorite professors showed up unexpectedly one day and ordered burgers with fries and beer. For the next two months, they came back every Friday. I assumed they'd merely discovered some burgers they were crazy about.

It would be years before I realized they were more concerned about my well-being than they were about the lunchtime fare. They'd decided that a casual weekly check-in wasn't a bad idea until I fully regained my bearings. I also discovered that Mal followed up Friday lunches with a quick call to my parents, regularly assuring them that I was, and would be, fine. Years later, Mal finally fessed up that my old job as a research assistant had already been filled by the time I returned. He had gone to great lengths to talk the administration into a temporary data analyst position to keep me partially engaged in academics.

By winter break, the bar scene was less fulfilling and Mal

and I were discussing new and exciting research projects every Friday after lunch. By spring, Mal had to tell the same administrator he'd talked into having me back that he'd accepted an offer from Emory. He matter-of-factly asked if I would like to join him and continue on as a research assistant, making certain to point out the number of student bars in Atlanta before adding that they also had a decent doctoral program.

I followed Mal to Atlanta where, back in the saddle, I racked up a few prime-time scholarships and awards along my way to a doctorate. Three short years later, I accepted a professorial position at a major university and was well on my way to a successful career.

Mal and I continued our successful collaboration for decades. We worked together best when we focused on our research and the immediate tasks ahead. When a grant proposal or manuscript was rejected by our harshest colleagues, Mal would momentarily bemoan their negative feedback, then immediately begin the rewrite. His confidence and unwavering perseverance were contagious.

We never discussed my dismal failure at Northwestern. Rather than give me a professor's lecture on career advancement, he subtly dusted me off, helped me find my hat, and propped me up until I could give it another go. It's thanks to him that I became equipped to face failure and rise up, willing to try again.

ADDICTION

CHAPTER FIVE

There's no other way to put it: I'm a human pig-sty. Maybe that's why Nellie bucked me to the ground. Can't say I'd blame her, either.

Musty arena sand and gravel have mixed with skunk juice, horse medicine, manure, urine, saliva, and perspiration to create a smell I've never experienced before. I can't stand myself any longer. Water and soap are the only remedy. So where can I undress and clean up without unduly contaminating the house?

The sofa is still on the front porch, partially blocking the door, so entering the house there is less than ideal. The garage entrance is more private, and I can disrobe there and avoid bringing additional filth and stench into the house.

I move deeper into the garage between Betty's black Lexus and my red pick-up truck, heading straight for the rusty old fridge on the back wall. June's mid-day heat is continuing to beat down, and the fridge contains at least a case of ice cold Yuengling—the best beer Pennsylvania ever made.

The spare fridge and the beer within suddenly become a greater obstacle to entering the house for a shower than the sofa on the front porch. Half of a bottle of Yuengling is gone before I figure out what to do with the twist top in my hand. I stick it in the pocket of my jeans as I ponder the effort necessary to take off my boots and eventually my pants. Perfectly fitting cowboy boots are comfortable to wear but a pain to get on and off. My tight jeans, purchased ten pounds ago, won't be any easier.

I get tired just thinking about removing the boots and jeans. Rationalizing the need to sit and take a short break, I grab a second Yuengling without finishing the first and head back around the house to the front porch with the smelly sofa. Fortunately, the skunk smell doesn't completely overwhelm me as I move toward the non-contaminated end. Under any other circumstances, I wouldn't think of sitting on the new sofa in this nasty condition, but I figure it's already ruined, so I plop down while swigging the last of the first bottle. I immediately start on the second.

The day is getting warmer and the second beer has gone down as easily as the first. Now I have an important decision. Do I get a third? The third will increase the probability of a fourth, which does the same for a fifth, and eventually the odds are in favor of putting a six-pack under my belt. If so, I'll be useless the rest of the day.

"To hell with it," I mutter under my breath. "The day's shot anyway." It is, after all, *my* Father's Day.

Back in the garage, I reach for the fridge door to get the third beer. I place one hand on the fridge door and the other on the base of the fridge and slowly pull my hands away from one another so that the fridge opens silently. I recognize this as my signature "quiet move," used late at night to keep Betty in the dark about my midnight grazing. No need for such deception today, but the behavior is so ingrained. The residual guilt of this learned behavior causes me to momentarily rethink the third beer.

According to the dreaded "charts," my six-foot frame is at least 32 pounds heavier than is ideal. In my younger days, I could shed a handful of pounds by skipping a lunch or two and jogging a modest distance a couple of days a week. It's become much harder with age. In the voice regularly used to address college freshmen three rows back in her introductory classes, Betty informs me that one's metabolism decreases with age. If I'm totally honest with myself—and when it comes to food and drink, I am not—I will admit that metabolism is a miniscule part of the problem. I've always liked to eat and always liked to drink. I used to like to exercise, but not so much anymore. Most importantly, I just don't care as much as I once did.

I should be worried about my health, but I don't seem to be. Others seem to be conscious of their looks. Me? Not so much. I've gradually grown satisfied with whatever my weight is. My self-image seems to recalibrate as I expand.

Betty was already a nutrition professor when I met her. I was immediately smitten, notwithstanding her area of expertise. Looking to learn as much about her as possible, I would sneak into the back of the large lecture halls where she taught. I thought of it as doing as much reconnaissance as possible before asking her out. Today, it would probably be labeled stalking and she would have me escorted out by campus security.

I fondly recall her style, grace, and intelligence as a lecturer, and especially the content of a specific lecture I saw her deliver. She explained the culturally common phenomenon of gaining almost a pound or so a year as one ages. Lower metabolism and reduced activity together are the primary culprits. Like all invincible twenty-five year olds, I'd thought to myself, and later assured her, "That won't be me." Here I am, 30 years and at least 30 pounds later. For so many reasons, I hate that she was right.

At some point every year, I commit to losing weight and getting in shape. As is the case with most people, New Year's is often my spark. Each year, the length of time committed to watching what I eat and increasing exercise seems to diminish. This past year, I think I lasted a week. I just seem to care less each year. My latest rationalization is that if I have to live a life devoid of the pleasures of lazy days with great food and drink, I don't want to live long anyway.

Along with learning to open the fridge very quietly late at night and confirming the gradual weight gain that sneaks up on many of us, I've experienced one other nutritional truth—the role of alcohol in weight gain. The calories in the beer are only part of what associates it with a protruding belly. Lost inhibition accounts for the rest. I close the fridge after retrieving the third beer and find myself tiptoeing into the back door of the farm house with my dirty cowboy boots still on to retrieve an unopened bag of potato chips from the pantry.

I'm tempted to turn on the television and immerse myself

in the sedentary demands of watching a glacially-paced baseball game. It's mid-afternoon, I haven't eaten a thing all day, and the only thing that has worked out today has been a moral victory over Nellie following her effort to kill me. Why not eat the entire bag of chips, drink as much Yuengling as I want, and watch all nine innings of the Pirates and Indians in the air-conditioned comfort of the family room?

The sofa's absence from the family-room reminds me of at least one reason that's not a good plan.

I contemplate how quickly the skunk scent transferred from the dog to the sofa and decide that it isn't a great idea to sit on anything that hasn't already been soiled, especially my favorite recliner. I consider sitting on the floor in the open space left by the missing sofa, but decide that the carpet shouldn't be exposed to my condition any more than the recliner. There's only one comfortable sitting spot that matches my stench, and it's on the front porch. I head in that direction, passing through the garage and by the fridge one more time. Might as well grab the rest of the six pack. I'm kidding myself to believe I won't be back for it anyway.

The first two beers quenched my thirst. Now I'm just consuming alcohol in the middle of the day. The third, then fourth beer go down almost as quickly as the first two.

Nellie, Star, and Prissy continue to graze in the front pasture. They focus intently on the spot of grass directly in front of them, occasionally swishing their tails, then slowly moving forward to reach the next preferred clump. Typically, Nellie and Eugene are the only two horses allowed to graze in the front "show pasture." The other horses we board are kept out back. With Eugene isolated in his stall, Nellie is happy to have new company in her lush pasture.

Pasture management is a tricky thing, especially when the pasture doubles as your front yard. Too many horses will eat the grass short but leave patches of unattractive, less tasty, and tender weeds. Horses put out on the pasture when it is too wet from the spring rains will leave deep hoof prints that tear up the grass. Under the best of circumstances, the pasture grass thins in the summer months, and inevitably there are bare spots like the one Nellie slid through in our game of chicken earlier in the day.

Watching the tranquil grazing from the front porch on this warm Sunday afternoon adds to the intoxicating effect of the beer. My eyes grow heavy. I stretch out on the sofa, extending my still-booted feet toward the spot where Bo initially tried to hide in a curled-up ball. I discount the possibility that the residual skunk juice could permanently foul my working cowboy boots of five years.

Something in the grass catches my eye. No more than 40 feet away, a winding dark line is moving across the yard. My skin immediately tingles and my eyes widen. There's no mistaking that slithering motion through the grass. It's the snake! I hate snakes, and especially this one.

When we bought the farm, the previous owner was quick to tell us, with intense pride, about the nearly seven-foot long water snake he had purposefully put into the fishing pond next to the barn several years prior. The snake's job was to keep down the frog population. Apparently, too many pond frogs make for a raucous summer evening for humans trying to sleep with the windows open, or so he said.

I've seen the snake's walnut-sized head floating eerily in the water a couple of times, but I've never seen his monstrous body—until now. I see it slide through the grass, making its way across the front lawn toward the pond.

Betty and I aren't bothered by the sound of frogs, and we'd certainly trade the slithering reptile for nightly serenades. We aren't inclined to sleep with the windows open during the Ohio summer anyway, not when we can use air conditioning instead. The monster snake in our pond has to go, but we haven't been able to craft an elimination plan. Betty hates snakes as much as me, and has not set foot in the tall grasses along the sides of the pond since the first sighting of the serpent's head.

I jump to my feet, deciding to take immediate action.

Granddaddy was quick to take a rake or a hoe to an unwanted reptile and could usually finish the job in one quick strike. In his mind, all snakes were unwanted. I want to do the same, but I'm kept at bay by a fear-inspired lack of confidence that I'll be able to get close enough to kill it with a hoe. The snake's body is substantially longer than the hoe handle, and if the snake begins wrapping itself around the handle, the situation will leave me with further soiled clothing. The best method of killing something from a distance, I decide, is a gun.

Unlike all of our rural neighbors and relatives, I'm not a

gun guy. I shot them while growing up, and I've been hunting once or twice, but we aren't into guns. Betty would be much more afraid of the gun than the snake.

I've almost resolved to find the hoe when I suddenly remember Grandpa Bob's old gun—his .32 caliber revolver. I agreed to take my turn storing it a few years back. It has been passed secretly around the family for decades in an effort to keep it away from Grandpa Bob and from those who might return it to him. My older brother handed it off to me when he started a late-life second family a couple of years back and did not want to keep it in the house with young children. I reluctantly climbed a chair and buried it in the far recesses of a side wall cabinet in the garage at our former house. When we moved to the farm, the gun went right back into the corner of a similar garage cabinet.

Now, standing on the same chair, I reach well back onto the upper shelf of the cabinet, as far back as I can along the side wall, and barely get a two-fingered grasp on what feels like the heel of a sock. As I gather the fabric with my fingertips, I begin to explore the outline of the object it contains. Indeed, it is a small pistol. A dingy white athletic sock with two thin-blue stripes around the top holds the gun and two bullets.

The gun looks to be in good shape—no rust, and obviously oiled in the recent past. I open the cylinder, make certain it is empty, close the cylinder, then point the revolver high in the air before pulling the trigger. The hammer seems to strike the firing pin as designed.

I inspect each bullet, remembering what my Aunt Debbie

said when she passed it along to my brother: "Dad hasn't shot this thing in decades. He kept these bullets in the sock, but I can't be certain they even go with this gun."

"Did Grandpa Bob have other guns?" I asked.

"No, not that I know of," she responded.

I remember thinking, *Why would he put bullets for another gun in the sock with this one?*

Aunt Debbie added, "I certainly wouldn't shoot it without having it checked out by a professional. They told me a few years back that the barrel might explode."

Now, the bullets don't look too bad, but a fine line of rust is visible between the casing and the lead of the actual bullet on each cartridge. I open the six-bullet revolving cylinder and load the two bullets into adjacent chambers. Even though I'm in a hurry to get back to the snake—he must be getting close to the pond by now—I can't resist spinning the cylinder like a cowboy before closing it tight.

I've not had any previous desire to fire Grandpa Bob's gun. The opportunity to eliminate the snake, assisted by liquid courage supplied by the beer, has moved me to action. I'm on a mission, possibly an ill-advised one, fueled by beer and implemented with a potentially dangerous and faulty weapon.

When I catch up with it, the snake is still about twenty feet from the edge of the pond. Sensing the water before him and my approach from behind, he increases his slivering pace and whips through the grass.

I'm close enough to hit him with a hoe. Now nervous

about the old gun, I wish that's what was in my hand.

Aim right between his eyes, I tell myself.

Getting down into the position I've seen cops use on TV—legs spread, both arms forward, one hand on the gun itself, supported by an overlaid non-trigger hand—I simultaneously squeeze the trigger and close my eyes. The hammer clicks but the gun doesn't fire. My hands recoil instinctively, but without cause.

Was it a dud? I quickly ask myself before remembering the act of spinning the cartridge. The bullets could be anywhere in the cylinder.

Frustrated and embarrassed at my carelessness in loading the gun, I'm fully prepared to let the serpent escape. Still in half-hearted pursuit, I see him unexpectedly stop at the edge of the water and raise his head to survey the landscape. Five feet away, with gun in hand, I am suddenly paralyzed by his size and presence. He's at least seven feet long, with the largest part of his body as big around as a hard salami. I ease forward, regaining my composure, the gun in my right hand trained directly between his eyes as he continues to scan the landscape of the pond's edge with his raised head. I'm close enough to see his thin forked tongue dart quickly and recede.

I lean toward him and, with the gun now less than three feet from his head, pull the trigger. A loud pop escapes the gun along with a light trace of smoke from the barrel. The bullet enters the pond water with a tiny splash about four inches from the shore. From the splash, I expect to be able to retrace the angle of the bullet back through a hole in the snake's head and up into the barrel of Grandpa Bob's firearm.

But the snake's head isn't where it was when I fired. Nor is it lying in the green grass, lifeless, with a hole in its center. Rather, the head is fully submerged and the first three feet of its body has already entered the pond. As the tail passes, I stomp at it with my foot, missing it as well. The snake slips under the water without leaving a ripple.

I must've at least grazed him, I try to convince myself. *Or maybe the rusty bullet didn't have enough remaining power to penetrate the snake's head.*

A walnut-sized head surfaces in the center of the pond to answer my questions. It cruises effortlessly across the surface, surveying its domain in a victory lap around the small pound. To at least disrupt his smugness, I'd like to take a wild shot from a distance, but decide to save the bullet, assuming there is an active bullet remaining.

When I check my hand and realize that the gun fired and didn't explode, I allow myself to reframe the incident as a small victory. Then, despair.

"How could you miss from three feet?" I ask myself. "Must have been a bad bullet! Or at least a crooked barrel!"

But I am not convinced by my own defense.

"You should have used the damn hoe," I mumble.

I never allow myself to consider the role of four bottles' worth of alcohol in my decision to use an antiquated, untested gun with rusty bullets to fire at the walnut-sized head of a moving snake.

I'm still mumbling to myself, louder now and blaming

everything except myself, as I make it back around to the front porch, stretch out on the soiled sofa, and reach for the fifth beer.

"What a crappy day!" I shout at the top of my lungs.

Friday, December 24, 1965

Pop stared down at the plate in front of him. The table was arranged perfectly for a Christmas Eve dinner—five matching plates, accompanying flatware, and napkins. Sam and I were sitting in front of two of the other plates on the worn wooden table. We were in the large kitchen and dining area of the aging farmhouse.

I watched Pop sit patiently in the shadows of the dimly lit room, knowing he had been in this position so many times. Mom stood in front of the dated gas stove, stirring butter beans and periodically opening the oven door to check on the fried chicken and rolls being kept warm. We had fully cooked the meal at our home before we made the 27-mile drive out to the old homestead, my dad's birthplace.

The homestead was a three-room cabin with a combined kitchen and dining area, a bedroom, and a front "parlor" with wood burning stove. The fireplace and gas oven in the kitchen were the only forms of heat in the plank board structure, built in 1919. The house only got running water and electricity in 1958, and the bath house, containing the toilet, a claw-footed tub, and an open shower with floor drain, was located in a small separate building, only accessible via a catwalk connecting it to the back porch.

Mom's persistent peeks into the oven were part nervousness, part concern for how the carefully prepared food was faring in the dilapidated oven. No doubt she feared rolls as hard as baseballs and chicken as dry as leather.

Headlights suddenly shone through the dingy curtains on the front windows, casting their recognizable pattern along the back wall of the kitchen. Pop, Sam, and I tensed a bit but didn't move. Mom stirred the butter beans faster.

A car door opened and closed a few long moments later. Heavy boots plodded slowly up the porch steps.

The front door swung open and a tall lanky man with thin white hair staggered a few steps into the front room, his work cap in one hand and a two-thirds empty bottle of Old Grand Dad bourbon whiskey in the other. The image of a sixty-five-year-old widower appearing two hours late and sopping drunk for a special homemade Christmas Eve dinner with his son's family was, for me, memorable, and the aptly named whiskey in his hand unforgettable.

Pop was still staring into his plate when Grandpa Bob made his way into the kitchen. Leaning against the door frame, he took a long swig of whiskey directly from the bottle, prioritizing the nip over saying hello or extending a welcome.

"Well, lookee what we got here," was his cordial greeting to the family as soon as he finished swallowing the whiskey.

"Hi, Grandpa Bob," I said cheerily, rising from my seat and anticipating a hug. Pop's arm extended quickly and gently directed me back into my chair.

Grandpa Bob completely ignored me and headed slowly across the kitchen, directly toward my mom. Mom stared into the pot of butter beans as if searching to remove any unwanted pieces of hull. Sam, who better understood the situation, remained perfectly still.

Grandpa Bob shuffled across the room, stopping long enough to toss his tattered cap onto the plate Pop continued to intently examine. Pop didn't flinch, refusing to be baited into a reaction.

Sauntering up behind Mom, Grandpa Bob draped the whiskey bottle over her left shoulder while reaching around her with his right arm to stick his hand into the beans and pluck one out with his fingertips. He held the bean close to her cheek for a moment, inspecting it while it cooled, then carefully bit just the tip with his front teeth before flicking the remains back into the pot.

With his putrid whiskey breath, he frowned and hissed directly into her ear, "Your ol' mean mama sure didn't teach you much!"

Like Pop, she didn't flinch.

Grandpa Bob somehow managed, without falling, to lower himself into a chair next to Sam. Pop, seated at the end of the table, removed the old cap from his plate and dropped it onto the planked floor. Grandpa Bob carefully placed his forearms on the edge of the table and clasped his fingers together over his plate, his chin raised high, mocking the formality of the place-setting with a smirk.

Mom moved more quickly now, taking the sheet of fried chicken from the oven and placing it directly on the table along with the now hardened rolls. Likewise, the beans came directly to the table in the pot—no hot pads tonight. The battered wood on the worn table wouldn't suffer any unfamiliar scarring from the scalding pot.

Patience was running thin, and haste was warranted in getting this affair over with. Eight p.m. was rapidly approaching and we'd been in the farmhouse for almost three hours, waiting for Grandpa Bob to come home. Had it been a surprise visit, there might have been more tolerance for the delay and the condition of his arrival. It hadn't been. He had confirmed our plans by phone the previous night—a sober Thursday!

Ironically, Grandpa Bob insisted on blessing the meal. He bowed his head, fingers entwined, and launched into a sincere, impromptu prayer.

"We thank you Lord for this food and this family. You are the supreme and holy god. We humbly ask you for strength. Amen." For a moment, he sounded sober, then lowered his chin to his chest long enough for us to assume he'd passed out. Finally, he raised his head slowly, and without hesitation reached for a drumstick with one hand and the whiskey bottle with the other. He swigged the whiskey while waving the chicken leg like a 4th of July flag.

Sam and I were calmed by the thoughtful prayer and amused by the chicken leg-waving. We smiled at one another, confirming our mutual belief that Christmas Eve had taken a turn for the better.

With fingers on each end of the drumstick, Grandpa Bob slowly rotated the piece as he inspected Mom's fry work. Finding the perfect spot, he bit through the golden crust, overdramatically tearing off a chunk with his teeth, and chewed.

Sam was reaching for a roll, and Pop the butter beans, when Grandpa Bob suddenly lunged over his plate and across the width of the table, extended both arms to the side, and swiped from left to right like a windshield wiper.

Food flew!

His follow-through left him tumbling into Sam's chair and overturned his own. Sam landed on the floor atop the chicken and beans while rolls spun on their axes nearby. Grandpa Bob grabbed the edge of the table with both hands and managed to finish the move partially upright, resting on one knee beside the table.

Sheepishly, he proclaimed, "Driest damn chicken I ever tasted!"

Mom began to weep. I sat petrified.

Pop sprang into action. First, he helped Sam off the floor while scanning for injury. Then he turned to his father.

From his kneeling position, Grandpa Bob glanced up inquisitively as Pop moved in behind him, kicking his overturned chair out of the way. Approaching from the rear, Pop reached down with an open hand and grabbed the back of Grandpa Bob's loose-fitting work pants where they gathered at the belt. In one smooth powerful motion, he lifted him to his feet.

Grandpa Bob steadied his upper body with hands still on the table. With one hand still grasping the back of his drunken father's trousers, Pop placed his other hand on Grandpa Bob's shoulder and firmly directed him away from the table.

Grandpa Bob remained silent and passively allowed himself to be steered around the mess on the floor. His only unassisted motion was to grab the bottle from the table. Flinching just a bit as Pop cinched his pants higher with a twist of his fisted hand, Grandpa Bob watched his own feet shuffle as he was disrespectfully pushed toward his bedroom. Had he been in a sober state, it would have been uncomfortable and demeaning. But Grandpa Bob didn't seem the least bit embarrassed.

As the room fell silent, Pop leaned forward and spoke directly into his father's ear. "You ruined my childhood. You won't ruin my children's."

Like Pop, Grandpa Bob wouldn't be baited into a response.

Sam and I tried to calm ourselves and help Mom remove the food and dishes from the floor. We hastily dumped everything into the sink—pots, chicken, pans, butter beans, plates, rolls, even napkins. Mom used a broom to quickly sweep up what she could.

The room was still a mess when Pop returned to the kitchen. The floor was clear but would need considerable mopping before becoming safe to cross. Miraculously, Grandpa Bob's plate was still on the table, populated only by a drumstick with a single bite missing.

"Boys, go get in the car," was all he said.

We wasted no time scrambling out of the room toward the front of the house, but like rubberneckers passing a car wreck, we couldn't resist slowing down to peer into Grandpa Bob's open bedroom door. He was lying in his bed with pillow propped behind his head, taking another swig. Had Pop really taken care to prop a pillow behind the old drunk's head?

"What the hell are you little peckerwoods looking at?" Grandpa Bob howled when he looked up to see us ogling him. "Damn kids! Where the hell did all these damn kids come from?" he ranted. "I can't stand it! Little turds everywhere!" I remember wondering if he'd forgotten spawning eleven kids himself.

Paralyzed once again, Sam and I stood in front of the doorway until Pop's firm hands on our shoulders gently prompted us toward the front door.

We rushed down the steps and piled into the back seat of the car while Pop and Mom locked Grandpa Bob in his own house. His ranting could still be heard through the panes of glass in both car and house as we drove away.

Pop said very little en route to our house. Mom tried to help us, her nine and eleven-year-old sons, understand what they had just witnessed. She told us stories about Grandpa Bob's difficult life. She told us how alcohol makes people act in ways they wouldn't act normally. She told us about our loving grandmother, how she had died years ago, and how it had changed Grandpa Bob.

As soon as our AMC Rambler rolled to a stop in our driveway, the explanation ended and the episode was over. We wouldn't discuss it as a family again.

That night, Santa Claus brought a new Fender electric guitar to two boys too old to still believe in such things. Sam and I had been taking guitar lessons on a classic starter guitar, but longed for an instrument that would propel us from folk to rock-and-roll. The beautiful white guitar and suitcase-sized amplifier were strategically placed in front of the tree—unwrapped, plugged-in, and ready to strum.

When we raced into the room, Pop was sitting in his favorite chair drinking his early morning coffee. We whooped and hollered and admired the gifts in tandem. Sam held the base as I inspected the neck and frets. Then, after swapping ends, we shifted to the amp. Within minutes, Sam was sitting on the floor directly in front of Pop, our audience of one, hesitantly sounding out the chord scheme to the Beatles' hit song "Help." He definitely needed help.

We opened dozens of presents that morning. Mom got a griddle that made her cry. Sam and I were flattered. We wouldn't understand the meaning of the tears until we married women who didn't mind explaining what constituted an acceptable gift and an unacceptable one. Pop received the obligatory tie with accompanying rack to hang in his closet.

Working in concert with Santa, Mom and Pop had wrapped a colorful guitar strap, a capo, extra strings, and music books with the chord patterns for our favorite songs.

Finger picks of various size and shape mixed with the candy in our stockings.

We paid little attention to the socks and underwear that we assumed were wrapped as filler presents to assure appropriate volume under the tree. We failed to recognize these presents as Pop's only shout-out to his own father. Years later, long after Grandpa Bob's death, we would hear Pop end nearly every story about his notorious dad's bad behavior with, "but . . . he always made certain we had new socks and underwear at Christmas."

Unlike the multitude of salient events shaping my composite, positive view of Gus, my memory of Grandpa Bob was grounded in that bizarre Christmas Eve. Other relatives would relate different, more positive, stories about Grandpa Bob, but the picture they painted was of a man I never saw.

I couldn't really remember Grandpa Bob's wife, my grandmother. The two had produced nine boys and two girls. That was fact.

The rest of his life story was delivered to us in a combination of selective memory and reconstructive history, its tone and content depending completely on the storyteller. By most accounts, he worked five days a week and was sober until the whistle blew on Friday afternoon. From the Friday closing until sometime during the middle of Sunday night, he stayed drunk. Monday morning, he showed up religiously for work, never late, and never missing a day.

My grandmother raised the eleven children and lived long enough to meet all of her 31 grandchildren and half a dozen great-grandchildren. Nonetheless, she had started early, and she died young at 57.

Half the family framed it this way: "Grandpa Bob fell apart after Grandma's death and became a mean, bitter drunk." An equal number of family members framed it, "Grandpa Bob was a mean, bitter drunk and drove Grandma to her grave." None could deny the abuse. Only the origins were in question.

Some could cite very specific instances and recounted them repeatedly as a means of catharsis. Others coped by repressing negative memories. Pop told of trying to wave his father's car down for a ride while walking the three miles home following afterschool baseball practice; Grandpa Bob would routinely pass him by as he drove home from work. At home, Pop would say, "Dad, I tried to wave you down for a ride."

"You should have taken the bus," was his reported response.

The most egregious behavior described to us involved Grandpa Bob riding to town on Saturday mornings with Grandma and any children still living at home but too young to stay by themselves. Those old enough to stay alone were smart enough not to get in the car. Grandpa Bob, already halfway through a bottle when they arrived in town, would head straight for his favorite bar. Grandma would have taken most of his cash for groceries, leaving him just enough for his liquor. If he had enough for his whiskey, he didn't question other expenditures. If he didn't have enough, he was violent.

Grandma would take the children to the grocery and buy food for the week. By noon, she would have completed any other miscellaneous chores and returned to the car. Grandpa Bob wouldn't return to the car until they cut him off at the bar, usually just after dark.

Pop's siblings sometimes told of Grandpa Bob in happier, younger times. Older siblings periodically told of him playing the fiddle and being the life of the party. Others remembered him cheering them on at high school athletic events.

Pop remembered sweltering August Saturdays in the backseat of a car with two crying younger siblings, waiting for Grandpa Bob to be thrown out of a bar. That suppressed any possibility of positive recollections.

FORGIVENESS

CHAPTER SIX

Warm water trickles from above, and a wet washcloth brushes lightly across my cheek. But as I slowly open my eyelids, I realize there's no shower—only Lola's pink tongue rhythmically lapping gently against my cheek. Steady rain from an afternoon shower falls on the roof and the full metal downspouts on each end of the porch mimic shower water.

I'm still stretched out on the soiled sofa, trying to determine how long I've slept, when a thunderous clap instantly completes my awakening. Sparks fly from the top of the utility pole out by the main road. Lola cowers and whines next to the couch. Bo must be hiding somewhere else.

"You've got to be kidding," I say to Lola, as if she could have miraculously prevented the transformer from blowing. The last time it happened, it was two days before we regained electricity on the farm.

Gathering myself to assess the damage from both beer and storm, I survey my near environs to find the empty bag of chips on the concrete porch slab, next to the fifth and sixth empty beer bottles. A bit groggy, I pull my phone from my pocket to check the time, forgetting that the battery is dead. When did I give up my simple, reliable wrist watch for the much less reliable clock that resides on the phone?

I have no idea how long I've napped. Mostly coherent,

and feeling only residual effects from the afternoon alcohol, I estimate that it's been a couple of hours. Noting the empty bottles surrounding me on the porch, I'm immediately ashamed.

Every morning for the past few years, I've made myself a promise when I rise. I won't drink today! I've broken that promise most days, but usually not until well after sundown, when the beer or wine fades into bedtime. Today I managed to disappoint myself early. I pick up each of the bottles and experience an even deeper disdain for my lack of restraint. The bottles fit nicely into the empty bag of Lays potato chips.

The afternoon shower is subsiding. I hustle through the remaining drizzle carrying the empties around to the garbage can in the garage. By instinct, I do more than just open the lid and set the bag on top. As I've done hundreds of times, I push it deep into the garbage to further hide the evidence already concealed in the chip bag.

I try to recall the events that led to my unintended nap, and the vivid image of the snake slithering into the pond suddenly emerges.

"The gun!"

I dash back around to the porch as if someone could have sped down the drive without my noticing and discovered my misdeeds. The pistol is lying on the front step, and its carrying case, the dingy white sock, peeks out from under the corner of the soiled sofa. Quickly retrieving the gun, I carefully open the six-shooter's cylinder. As I remove the two shells, I discover that one is now an empty casing, and the other still contains its lead bullet. Upon further inspection of the unfired bullet, it's clear that the firing pin actually made contact with the cartridge, leaving a distinct impression in the soft metal button that activates the gunpowder. Indeed, it was a bad bullet.

It could just have easily exploded in the barrel, and may yet go off, I think to myself.

I immediately walk over to the pond and toss the empty casing and full cartridge into the deepest section. I return the gun safely to its sock and hiding place in the back of the garage storage cabinet, vowing to keep the snake-hunt story to myself and hoping to do a better job of keeping that commitment than my daily alcohol promise.

As I exit the garage, the sun majestically breaks through the clouds. The shower has cooled and cleansed the afternoon, and the distinct after-shower freshness immediately draws my attention back to the pond. The aerator that usually bubbles continuously in the center of the pond is silent, confirming my theory of the blown transformer and providing a reminder that we'll be without electricity for some time.

There's nothing I can do about that, but electricity is certainly not required for catching fish. The fishing is always best in the early morning and late afternoon; it's a little early in the day to be ideal, but the fish also bite immediately, and in good numbers, after a late-spring squall.

The mirrored surface of the pond shows no evidence of the snake—not even a head or beady little eyes. It's either beneath the surface or escaped out onto a rock to enjoy the returning sun. Out of sight is not necessarily out of mind, and I continue to wonder and worry about the snake's whereabouts.

Nonetheless, the still pond is alluring. Recently mown green grass surrounds nearly two-thirds of its kidney shape. The other third of the pond's perimeter is populated with pussy willows and cat tails. The pond is easily accessible for fishing and is well-stocked.

The previous owners kept largemouth bass and bluegills and referred to them as pets. Both breeds were, and are, well fed daily, with fish food from the local farm and garden store. As the new owner, I had assumed the responsibility of taking our pets out of the water occasionally to fully demonstrate my concern for their well-being, and thus I fish almost every day.

The largemouth bass are plentiful and up to 18 inches long. They are quick to bite and, once hooked, inclined to fight frantically for their freedom. The bluegills are much shorter, but are also thick, and ounce for ounce pull harder and more consistently. I routinely entertain myself by catching a few, reminding them who provides them food and water, then returning them to the pond to be caught another day.

This style of fishing is enhanced by living on a horse farm where there is an abundance of worms. Worms thrive in decomposed horse manure, and there's obviously plenty of that here. The manure "cooks" until it becomes fine compost, which naturally attracts worms. I maintain my very own worm farm at the edge of the pond by periodically refreshing the compost in a buried wash tub covered with an oval piece of half-inch plywood. A little corn meal once a week and there's never a need to hit the bait shop for fat, juicy worms.

The work shed attached to the barn is conveniently located within hosing distance from the south edge of the pond. (The initial reason for digging the pond was to assure that water was available to fight potential barn fires.) The first owners' use of the pond as a home for the "pets" was secondary. Its current use as recreational fishing is all my idea, but the pond's proximity to the barn makes the front corner of the shed a perfect spot for storing my fishing rods and tackle box.

I keep three identical ultra-light rods with fine two-pound test line in a homemade rod holder just inside the door of the shed. The small flexible rods and delicate open-faced reels are all rigged with a tiny gold hook, a half-ounce slip lead, and a three-quarter inch round bobber to let the hooks float freely in about 18 inches of water. Three fully prepared rods can accommodate a couple of occasional fishing buddies who might drop by, and save me valuable time should I need a backup rod when the fish are biting particularly well and one breaks the line.

Unlike most fishing environments, where travel and preparation can exceed actual fishing time, I simply grab a rod, walk a few feet to the worm bed, dig into the moist compost with my fingers to find a fat one, hook him twice, and drop a line.

The pond's shape and size is such that a strong cast from

strategic spots along the shore can reach nearly every nook and cranny that might house a fish. I've fished the pond enough to have the home field advantage of knowing where the largest fish reside most times of the day. One such spot is directly under the branches of the river birch tree that sits at the pond's west edge.

On hot afternoons with no prior rain, the only place you can catch a fish is the shade, where bugs might fall from the tree. On days like today, after the rain has created perfect conditions, the fish will bite almost anywhere. The biggest fish, however, are still likely to be lurking under the extended tree limbs.

The birch's location on the pond's periphery makes it a cinch to put the worm in the perfect location. With an underhanded flick of the rod and a quick thumb release of the line, I send the hook into the water just at the edge of the shadow created by an overhanging tree limb. The worm sinks quickly and the bobber hasn't fully settled from the small splash it created when it disappears completely under the water. The slack in the line tightens instantly and the tip of the pole bends dramatically toward the escaping fish as I realize the need to pull back against the assault, firmly setting the hook.

The limber rod doubles over immediately and the reel begins to sing as the lightly set drag allows several feet of the thin line to escape. Without warning, the pole suddenly pops back to its original straight line form as quickly as it doubled over. Six feet of thin line hangs freely out of the last eyelet on the end of the rod. The fish is gone, as are the hook, bobber, and sinker.

"Damn!" I say, stomping my foot in the still wet grass surrounding the pond.

Using a light rod and thin line, with the barb carefully smashed down on the hook, substantially increases the challenge and gives meaning to the fight. The fish still has a chance, even after making the decision to bite a baited hook. However, it's maddening when the light combination throws the odds too far in favor of what had to be one of the biggest fish in the pond. I really wanted to see that fish. Maybe the drag should have been set even lighter to allow the line to escape more freely. Maybe there was a flaw in the quality of the line, or it caught on one of the grommets on the rod. Maybe I simply yanked too hard and unknowingly jeopardized the catch.

Before I finish pondering the endless list of possible errors, something unexpectedly breaks the surface with a muffled sound like an expertly released Champagne cork.

The snake! is my first fleeting thought, but then I see the familiar red and white bobber settling on the surface about five feet from where the original strike occurred.

The lunker is either resting from the fight and hovering just under the surface, or the bobber escaped to the surface when slipping off the loose end of the broken line. Suspecting the latter, but hoping for the former, I reach out as far as I can with the end of the rod and use it to gently direct the bobber toward the shore.

New hope arises. With one knee in the grass on the edge of the pond and the other leg fully extended behind me for balance, it's possible to lean out and carefully grasp the bobber. I'm as prepared for a second fish fight as I can be in this awkward position. If the fish is as large as this optimistic fisherman is imagining, I could easily end up in the pond with the fish and, heaven forbid, the snake.

The momentary anticipation fades when the bobber lifts easily from the water. No line and no fish!

At least I've salvaged my red and white bobber, I think to myself.

I accept the moral victory, remembering that the tackle box will have plenty of hooks and weights, but I realize that I may be down to my last bobber. I smugly enter the shed now, for I know that two additional rods are rigged identically to the first. There should be no delay getting back into action.

But something isn't right with the remaining rods—something I didn't notice in the excitement of retrieving the first rod. The homemade wooden holder is nothing more than a couple of three-foot-long 2x4s mounted on the wall a foot apart, parallel to the ground and each other. The rods fit into notches such that they stand perpendicular to the ground but parallel to each other. The spot for the first rod is visible from the open door and is obviously empty. The other two rods are visible only after you come far enough into the shed to see behind the door.

Today, one rod is on the ground leaning up against the wall just under the holder, which is mounted at eye level. The other rod is lying across the top 2x4. I'm a little miffed that someone has used the rods and not neatly replaced them in their designated spots on the rod holder. I'm downright angry when I pick up each rod and discover its condition.

The rod that lies across the upper board of the holder looks much like the rod I just returned to the shed. Six feet of loose line hangs from its end—no hook, sinker, or bobber. I shake my head in disgust and place this rod in its proper position, not bothering to re-rig it.

The rod on the ground propped against the wall is in much worse shape. Like the first rod, there is no evidence that it was ever properly rigged, or poised to be the next weapon in my mini-arsenal. In addition to having no rigging, the open-faced reel has become a huge bird's nest of tangled line. The culprit? A novice user who doesn't know how to control the flow of reel-line with their thumb while casting. Also known as a "backlash," the reel spins faster than the line can escape and creates a jumbled mess of line that accumulates around the reel itself.

Untangling a serious backlash is nearly impossible. Most often it's easier to sacrifice whatever amount of line is involved and start over, which means rewinding new line, and that takes away a substantial amount of time from fishing.

The fish are biting, but I've lost a big one, and now my back-up rods and reels are in shambles.

"Who the hell did this?" I shout without expecting an answer.

Ironically, the rods are there for both back-up and for

others to use. I really enjoy seeing friends and visitors fishing in the pond, especially children and parents fishing together for the first time. I want them to use the equipment, and I keep plenty of well-fed worms close to the pond for that express purpose. I should realize that trashed equipment is one of the potential costs associated with sharing my resources with others, but the results in front of me are no less inconvenient and upsetting.

This is not the excusable work of children, I determine. We're careful to assure that visiting children are accompanied by adults when close to the pond. One of our biggest nightmares would be to have a child drown on our property. Consequently, we are diligent in requiring children close to the pond to be well-supervised.

I suddenly remember Max and the two girls out by the pond last weekend. Nine-year-old Stella and ten-year-old Harriett are the owners of the aging school horse named Macho Man who boards at our farm.

Like the ever patient Macho Man, I try to overlook the girls' rowdy nature, sympathetic as I am to their disrupted home life. Their mom, Sally, accompanies them to the farm most days with strong alcohol on her breath. She often retreats behind the barn "for a quick smoke," and I assume to hit the flask.

A slick guy named Max picks them up now and again, but rarely exits his second-hand BMW convertible, preferring to blow the horn to summon the kids for their ride home rather than taking a few minutes to help them with Macho Man.

His lack of involvement and rare out-of-car sightings make his pond appearance last week particularly memorable. I had noted his unusual presence, but busy with other chores, I didn't pay close attention to his activities. They must have been fishing.

Max immediately rises to the top of my list of suspects. I don't like him anyway! His disengaged impatience and sense of entitlement would lead to just this type of disrespect for my fishing system and property. To be fair, I don't really know Max, or that much about him. But he has to be the idiot responsible. I can think of no one else.

Each boarder's phone number is on a laminated placard on the horse's stall in case of emergency. Macho Man's reads "Sally Nordeski," followed by her cell number. Suddenly, I'm questioning whether this guy Max is really the father or if he even lives with this brood. I reach into my pocket and retrieve my phone, but can only stare into the black screen of the juiceless device. No battery, and now, with the power outage, no means to recharge it.

"What an ass," I mumble, uncertain whether I'm referring to Max or myself.

The tackle box is on top of the work bench in the shed, not its usual location on the shelf under the bench. I approach it to retrieve the tackle necessary to prepare a second rod and reel. It's clear that the one without the bird's nest will be first. The bird's-nest removal will be a much more involved process.

It's no surprise to find the tackle box a mess. The small

and varied compartments of a well-designed tackle box are ideal for obsessive organizers of hooks, weights, lures, flies, and all things fishing. Boxes for making beaded jewelry might be the only container to rival the organizational possibilities of a large tackle box.

I'm not an obsessive organizer, but I do like to have certain things in their appropriate place, especially fishing things. As it turns out, most of the tackle in my box has been randomly, and horrendously, rearranged. Compartments for lures contain bobbers. The bobber compartment has no bobbers, but now contains a random collection of hooks—big ones, tiny ones, barbed ones, unbarbed ones, gold hooks, and dull bronze hooks.

I am perversely relieved to find that the lead weights managed to survive the reorganization and are neatly arranged by weight, size, and shape in their homogeneous compartments. This small recognition of order is enough to distract me from wanting to harm Max. I refocus on rigging a second rod and getting back to the fish.

Given that I've put this same rig together hundreds of times and can literally do it with my eyes closed—except for putting the tiny two-pound test through the eye of a hook—it's not a major inconvenience to rig the rod. For an instant, I ponder why the two fouled rods and the one misarranged tackle box caused me such angst. Assuming Max was the culprit, I'd called him every name my head could muster. In truth, Max may have been completely innocent, and furthermore, it wasn't really such a grand transgression. I attribute my over-reaction to the day's cumulative misfortunes and the beer's lingering effects.

Back at water's edge with my back-up weapon now fully functional, I scan the surface quickly for the snake's head, unable to suppress a recent and recurring dream. In the dream, I'm fighting what I suspect is the biggest fish in the pond when the battle intensifies. With vicious vibration, the pole suddenly bends near the breaking point. I continue battling until the bobber clears the surface at the edge of the pond.

Bending over, I grasp the pole tightly in one hand and, with the other, prepare to land the fish by plunging my thumb into its open mouth at its connection with the hook. I reach toward the water, which breaks violently with the uncontrollable thrashing of a 20-inch largemouth bass wrapped in a slithering, shining mass of black coils. The dream always ends with a distinctive head peering up and pointing its darting forked tongue in my direction.

My skin crawls, but I bravely cast the line.

"It won't be long now," I say to myself, as I do with every cast. The bobber settles quietly on the surface about ten feet into the pond.

Last year's discarded Christmas tree is tied to a concrete block and lies on the bottom of the pond, directly under the bobber. I know, because I sunk it there just before the pond froze over last January. The protection the needle-less tree provided the tiny new minnows in the early spring drew in last year's feasting fingerlings, which immediately attracted the largest fish in the pond. I've caught a dozen or so in this exact spot, most well over a foot long.

The fish around the sunken tree often take the worm as soon as the bobber settles, and sometimes before. I'm fully prepared, with the rod tip up and eyes fixed on the bobber. A minute or two passes with no action. The bobber sits perfectly still in the same spot it was cast. This may take longer than I expected.

Noticing that the homemade plywood top is still off of the worm bed, I carefully lay the rod down in the grass with the tip at the water's edge and the rest extended perpendicularly back into the grass. I need to cover the worms before I forget, lest they dry out in the next day's sun, drown in its rain, or are picked off one-by-one by opportunistic robins.

As the ever vigilant fisherman, my eyes remain focused on the bobber while I grab blindly for the plywood lid. The bobber suddenly dips briefly below the surface, resurfaces for a fraction of a second, then disappears completely. The pole begins sliding through the grass, faster and straighter than the snake. I instinctively trap the rod to the ground with a quick sidestep of my right foot. The line is still escaping from the lightly set drag, but at least the pole won't slip into the water.

Retrieving the rod from under my foot in the grass is no problem. Averting this potential disaster provides me a slight ray of hope for landing the fish and salvaging the remainder of the day. Losing the entire rod and reel would have been par for the course given the day's events, but maybe things are looking up.

Grasping the rod at its base and placing my other hand on the reel's handle, I try to point the rod upward toward the sky. The base complies, but the tip continues to point toward the racing fish, thus creating a severe arc. For an instant, the line stops escaping. I manage to regain a tiny bit of it with quick cranks of the reel. Quickly lowering the tip for an instant and simultaneously cranking furiously allows me to gain a few more feet of line. Repeating this motion is successful and convinces me I've turned the fish toward the bank. Now it's only a matter of a few more cranks.

Suddenly, the fish breaks the water, his whole body thrashing as he tries to spit the hook. Like horses, fish can't really spit, so it's just a matter of creating such force and misdirection with their bodies that the barbless hook releases from the corner of their mouths.

I get a clear look at the fish and realize that it's not the biggest I've ever caught in the pond, and certainly not as big as the one that just got away. But it is a good-sized bass.

Quickly stepping away from the water's edge and raising the rod high while arching my back, I'm able to maintain tension on the line as the fish falls back into the pond, having expended a lot of energy with its jump. Suddenly, the fish hasn't much fight left in him. I reel him in against token resistance and land him without incident. The barbless hook slips easily from the side of his mouth and I throw him into the grass by the pond, far enough from the edge that he won't be able to flip and flop his way back into the water.

Given that it's my special day and that there'll be no cooking inside without electricity, I decide to eat what I've caught. This bass will be dinner.

It's a small win, but a win nonetheless, and I take it as a sign of a new direction for the disappearing day.

Saturday, May 10, 1962

Tap, tap, tap!

Sam, still in bare feet and pajamas at 6:30 a.m., stood on his tiptoes and gently knocked three times on Earl and Eloise's bedroom window with his tiny seven-year-old fist. He could barely reach the glass in the window of the one-story, three-bedroom house, no more than ten yards away from the car port of our adjacent home.

I didn't wait for a response at the window. As soon as he started knocking, I bolted the short distance across the grass to the entry next door.

Sam, older than me by sixteen months, easily passed me before I made it onto the small concrete pad serving as a front porch. We knew Earl would unlock and open the door by the time we got around front. Like nearly every Saturday morning of our young lives, we weren't disappointed.

Earl and Eloise lived next door in our modest Highland Terrace neighborhood in northern Florida. Eloise met Earl while working on the Navy base—he was on active duty. He would eventually retire and join her as a civilian worker on the same base, the two of them spending their entire lives in service to our country. Matched better by name than demeanor, Eloise stayed true to her prim and proper English upbringing while Earl never strayed far from his casual, laid-back Southern roots.

Our family moved into a newly built home in the neighborhood the same week that Earl and Eloise began to occupy theirs. I was only eleven months old, and promptly took my first step towards Eloise, a step that created a lifetime of friendship and support.

Several years older than my parents, Earl and Eloise had been unsuccessfully trying to have a child of their own. Sam and I became instant surrogates. By the time we were old enough to independently leave our beds on Saturday morning, reach the knob of the door leading from our house to the covered car port, and scurry across the grass to the bedroom window, we had created a special Saturday morning tradition.

Earl would let us in for our "morning coffee" while we waited for Eloise to rise and make pancakes on the griddle. The "coffee" was hot chocolate milk with a largely pretend splash of java. The silver-dollar sized pancakes were golden brown, and served in a pool of warm maple syrup with a tiny dollop of whipped butter. Needless to say, we rarely missed Saturday breakfast with Earl and Eloise voluntarily.

"How would you mullet heads like a little fishin' from the bay bridge?" Earl asked as soon as we both finished our last pancake. Mullet was the local fried fish of choice. The heads were unceremoniously tossed aside as they were cleaned; they were useless. Earl routinely, and lovingly, ribbed us with the label.

"Yay!" we yelled in unison, not bothering to respond to Earl's ribbing.

Earl loved to fish and had two very willing companions whenever he wanted to go. Sometimes we took his little aluminum fishing boat and cruised the bayous. Other times we fished off of the concrete retired bridge which, in its better years, had spanned the entire bay. After its retirement, the public bridge was used exclusively for fishing.

Earl began assembling the fishing gear while Sam and I ran home to get formal permission to go with Earl—formal in that we pretty much had blanket permission to spend Saturday mornings with Earl and Eloise. The folks got to sleep in and we had the full attention of doting adults.

Earl was already loading the truck with rods and reels, fishing boxes, and the cooler by the time we returned. Sam and I immediately noticed that we each already had a rod and reel loaded in the back of his light-blue 1957 Dodge truck. When he gave us the rod and reels the Christmas prior, Earl was adamant that we keep them at his house so he could make certain we didn't lose them and could be sure they were always rigged appropriately for the specific underwater prey we sought. After each outing, he rinsed the salt water from his equipment and ours, and saw to it that they were fully rigged and ready for the next time. We were delightfully spoiled little anglers.

Bridge-fishing was a popular Saturday morning activity in our small coastal town. The bridge's best spot was at the open end, where the remnants of what had once been the middle of the concrete span lay on the bay floor as shelter for fish. The bridge's center section was removed to allow larger boats to pass through after a new, much taller bridge was built and opened. Additional underwater "beds" had been created alongside other sections of the bridge using obsolete appliances, dried Christmas trees, and construction debris, though their exact location was sometimes hard to discern.

Vehicles drove all the way to the end of the mile-long ex-bridge before turning back toward land and parallel parking somewhere against the curb on the east side. Today, all of the parking spots at the very end were taken, which meant we would have to work our way back down the bridge and find a good spot closer to shore. Typically, the farther you went out on the bridge, the bigger the fish.

Earl said very little as he navigated past several potential parking spaces until finding the perfect one for his truck; it had enough room behind the extended tailgate to spread out our gear and cooler, but not quite enough room to park an entire vehicle in the space. The strategy, adapted from tail-gaiters at football game parking lots, would eliminate the possibility of another angler invading our space.

The rich folks in town fished from their well-equipped boats. The bay bridge was for much less affluent, but well-motivated, anglers. Earl's aluminum boat was great for the calm waters of the bayou, but couldn't handle the waves of the bay if a storm popped up.

"Boys, get out those shrimp. I hear that's what they're

biting on," Earl said, preparing the rigging on his favorite two rods-and-reels, both of which he'd packed for his own use.

"Sure," I offered, eager to help.

The shrimp were fresh from the bait store. Their heads were still on and their peppercorn black eyes protruded. I opened the container and carefully handed one shrimp to Sam and another to Earl, dubbing them Buster and Bubba before delivering them over to their fate. I would eventually get a line in the water, but first was eager to see if named shrimp would achieve better results as bait than unnamed ones. Sam was disgusted with the immaturity of it all. As with any of my antics, Earl found it amusing and rewarded me with his signature cackle and an open-handed slap to the side of his thigh. His laugh always made me smile.

Earl and Sam both cast their lines beautifully off the side of the bridge. Earl's precise cast was totally expected, but I was surprised that Sam, at seven, could thrust his line all the way into the bay, far away from the perilous rubble under the bridge.

Responding to an immediate tug, Earl yanked the tip of his pole toward the 10 a.m. sun. Nothing pulled back. He cranked the reel a couple of times and waited for another half-minute. No response. Patiently, he reeled in his hook and sinker and, as expected, found the shrimp stripped clean.

Meanwhile, Sam hooked a small croaker and had him out of the water, still flopping furiously and trying to escape during the twenty-five foot haul up to the bridge.

"See!" I shouted. "It worked. Buster and Bubba—great

shrimp!"

Sam looked in my direction with pure disgust as he removed the five-inch-long fish from the hook. The croaking sound coming from the fish now lying on the hot asphalt was true to its name. Croakers were fun to catch, but only the poor black people on the bridge ate them. Sam expertly slipped his thumb into the gills of the small fish as his pointer finger entered its tiny mouth. In one smooth motion, he flipped him into the plastic five-gallon paint bucket that Earl had lowered to the water on a rope to fill. The fish came to life and swam circles along the side of the bucket. We had no intentions of taking home a croaker, but would gladly give him to one of our fellow bridge-fishers more inclined to cook and eat him later.

I reached into the cooler containing the plastic bag full of fresh shrimp and unceremoniously flipped one in Sam's direction and another at Earl's feet. They were both anxious to bait their hooks and get their lines back into the water. Neither paid much attention to the nameless shrimp as they skewered them onto the hooks.

Earl's second cast was as perfect as the first. Sam had a little trouble, forgetting to release the line at the appropriate time as he swung the pole forward, causing the weight and line to flip back and wrap around the bridge's top railing. He moved quickly to untangle the mistake, hoping no one had seen. Like any respectable little brother, I immediately pointed out his error to Earl.

"I do that all the time," Earl said calmly as he set down his pole and helped Sam untangle his line.

Sam's next cast was perfect and he smugly glanced back over his shoulder in my direction. I nonchalantly looked away. Earl saw it all and smiled affectionately at us both.

This time their bait settled into the bay and they waited, and waited, and waited. After about ten minutes, Sam reeled his bait back up to the bridge but found it untouched. He whispered "Shorty" in the direction of the shrimp before casting it back out into nearly the same spot from which he had retrieved it. Earl followed suit, changing his bait and allowing me to name his shrimp Penelope.

While we were watching the motionless lines and pole tips, a brand new two-door Corvair coupe caught my attention as it zoomed past us and headed toward the end of the bridge. Earl looked over his shoulder, expressionless. This look was a change from his ever-present smile and good nature and clearly indicated his concern about a speeding car on a crowded bridge.

"Nice car," I said, admiring the stylish compact.

"We'll have to see how they hold up," was Earl's bland reply, knowing the Corvair was a new model.

The sports car continued on to the end of the bridge, swinging its rear end through the turnaround. Screeching rubber, it quickly accelerated back in our direction. Earl and Sam were still focused on their inactive fishing lines, but I looked back, startled at the sudden commotion as the Corvair barreled toward us. I was convinced it wouldn't stop until it was back on dry land.

As the Corvair arrived parallel to the car parked behind us, its driver laid on the horn and swerved dramatically into the tiny space we'd left. Earl quickly lunged from the rail, pulling me clear and tossing me as gently as possible onto the truck's tailgate. Sam squeezed tightly against the rail and closed his eyes. Tires screeched once again as the driver slid the little car into the tight spot, overturning the paint bucket with Sam's lone fish and sending part of our cooler sliding under the truck.

The driver shut off the ignition and swaggered out onto the pavement before the overturned paint bucket finished spinning. The little fish lay flopping in the resulting puddle of water, croaking like a bull frog.

"Catching anything?" the big, barrel-chested man asked casually, apparently unaware of any miscue.

He closed the car door behind him, taking time to wipe imaginary fingerprints from the door handle with the untucked tail of his bright yellow shirt.

Sam was cranking in his line furiously, likely anticipating a major confrontation. Earl walked deliberately toward the man, staring at him intently. With an unexpected smile, he said calmly, "Sorry our stuff was in your way. We would've made room if we'd had more time."

"Not to worry, good buddy," the man boomed, unaware of Earl's sarcasm.

Before Earl could respond, the whir of line leaving a reel caught our attention. Earl had propped his rod against the bridge rail before rushing to our protection. As he stood at the driver's side door with our new fishing buddy, the reel completely straightened up against the bridge rail. Earl dashed around the front of the car, while the big guy headed around the back. Both were intent on beating the other to the bending, whining reel.

As they approached the rod and reel from different directions, the handle lifted off the asphalt and began following the rest of the rod toward the top of the rail. The reel suddenly caught on the rail and the rig was momentarily suspended, its final plunge delayed.

Earl's hands were inches from the rod when the big guy crashed into his arms and upper body in his own attempt to save the rod and catch the fish. Earl fell to one knee, forced away from his favorite fishing rig. The big guy's hand grasped the air where the reel had hung just as it broke free and dutifully followed its tugging line toward the water's surface.

Earl, transfixed, watched the rod and reel all the way down and turned immediately to the big guy. Sam and I huddled together, expecting something horrible. We had never seen Earl lose his temper, but even young boys with limited experience in schoolyard scuffles could foresee the possibilities.

Earl's open hand extended and made solid and startling contact with the guy's back. His hand splayed against the yellow fabric as he moved closer to his side.

"Good try!" he said sincerely.

They both peered longingly into the dark water, as if they had both seen the last of a good friend.

"Sorry, man!" was all the big guy could say.

"That's why I bring a backup." Earl smiled, reassuring the man not to worry.

"Must have been a big one, eh?" Earl continued.

"Must have been," the big guy replied awkwardly before regaining his swagger and adding, "Gotta roll."

He was back in the Corvair and out of the tiny space as quickly as he'd slammed into it. With eerily similar pace and resolve, Earl retrieved his backup rod, now his primary rod, and asked me for a new shrimp.

"This is Big Bad Joe!" I exclaimed, moving confidently toward Earl and handing him the largest, ugliest shrimp in the plastic bag. Earl bellowed appreciatively and slapped his thigh.

Big Bad Joe yielded a nice-size croaker, as did every other named shrimp we put on a hook during the next hour. Sam caught four, Earl five, and I managed to pull myself away from naming shrimp long enough to snare one myself. We gave the croakers to the closest angler who expressed an interest and hadn't yet learned the value of naming shrimp.

Later that year, Earl was fishing in the same spot on the bridge when he hooked into something that put deadweight pressure on his line. Miraculously, the hook he was using caught in the last eye of the rod that had gone over the edge during the real Big Bad Joe fiasco. Whether through divine justice or not, Earl had his old rod and reel back. The reel was hopelessly rusted, but the rod was in perfect shape.

Earl told the story of Big Bad Joe well into my adulthood.

As the years passed, Big Bad Joe became a giant of a man, the little Corvair morphed into a Ferrari, and we caught five buckets of foot-long speckled trout. Sam and I never tired of the story.

Regardless of the growing exaggeration in the rest of the tale, Earl never uttered an unkind word about the rude intruder who nearly ran us over, invaded the sanctity of our fishing spot, and caused him to temporarily lose his favorite rod to the sea. Earl was the rare eternal optimist and positive soul who could find the good in everything and everybody.

Moreover, Earl could forgive.

When Sam and I mowed half of his yard before the lawnmower ran out of gas and failed to return to finish the job for three weeks, Earl told the neighbors he was experimenting with the length of grass he most preferred. Earlier that same spring, he paid us to weed his flower bed prior to its annual bloom. Not knowing a flower from a weed, we unearthed everything that was alive. Earl happily proclaimed that he and Eloise had been ready for a change in landscape for a long time.

Earl lived the saying our mothers all told us to follow: "If you can't say something nice about someone, say nothing at all."

If Sam or I lost an athletic event by an embarrassing margin, Earl as witness would frame it as "a close game." A disappointing report card, littered with B's and C's, was embraced as "just short of all A's."

As I aged, I must have disappointed Earl on countless

occasions. I'd come home from college with ample time to visit friends, but no time to check in for even a short visit or fishing trip with Earl. I must have missed his birthday more times than I can remember. Nonetheless, the next time our paths crossed, unconditional love and positive support prevailed.

There's a familiar joke that goes, "If you want to know who loves you more, your dog or your wife, put them both in the trunk of your car for thirty minutes and see which one is happy to see you when you let them out." My dogs express plenty of unconditional love and forgiveness, but I'd bet on Earl in that scenario every time.

DUTY

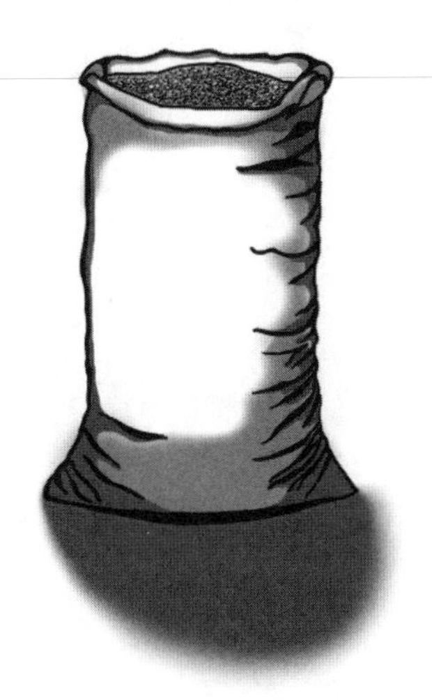

CHAPTER SEVEN

As my sharp fillet knife, held precisely against the grain, brushes briskly across the skin of the bass I've caught, the rapidly removed scales fly in every direction.

One scale lands flush on my cheek. I reassure myself that, come time for eating, the bass's delicate skin will be unbroken. Still not having showered, I don't bother to brush the scale off. What's one more smell? Besides, I depleted our entire supply of salt, vinegar, and even douche while dealing with the skunk and the hound.

I kneel and rinse the scaled fish at the edge of the pond, though I'm leery of the snake stealing it. With two fingers extended into the gills and the thumb of the same hand inserted into its mouth, I use my other hand to feel the skin for any lingering scales. Finding none, I place the fish back on a large flat rock at water's edge, and use the sharp knife to gut it from gills to tail, exposing its insides to be pulled out with my bare hand and tossed into the pond. No need to decapitate it. The bass will cook fine with the head on, just as the trout are at fancy mountain restaurants. One more careful rinse and it's ready for grilling.

I walk the fish over to the old fridge in the garage and carefully place it on a few folded paper towels from the roll hung nearby. The fish fits perfectly on top of the towels, right where the six pack sat this morning. Even with the electricity out, the old fridge will keep it cool enough for a few hours.

Since waking well over 12 hours ago, I've had coffee, a bowl of Cheerios, a big bag of potato chips, and six beers. I'm hungry for dinner, but a couple of obstacles stand in the way of a proper meal. The horses need dinner, and my dinner can't be easily prepared on an all-electric farm currently without electricity.

The horses, sans Eugene, are still out in the field. They must be retrieved, one by one, before they can be fed, and before I can prepare my own dinner.

"Damn!" I suddenly remember Eugene's grain gorge. The little he didn't consume was served for breakfast. It's nearly 6:00, and the feed store closed at 5:00. I'd made a mental note to get there between 1:00 and 5:00, but the damn beer interceded. (It's less shameful to blame it on the beer than the one drinking it.)

"Damn." It seems as if that's the word of the day.

The horses have been in the field all day leisurely eating lush, late-spring grass. They won't starve. But they won't readily accept an evening without grain. They'll spend the evening acting as if they're insatiably famished. Their kicking and chewing could cause immeasurable damage to their stalls and perhaps more to themselves. More importantly, there's explaining the empty grain can to Betty when she returns early tomorrow morning.

Even if the bins were full, Eugene wouldn't be getting any grain for dinner. He's been on stall-rest all day, with access only to water. I've checked his hooves every time I've passed the barn today. They haven't completely cooled, but they haven't become seriously hot, either. Still, the vet's instructions from the last episode were clear: No additional nutrients from grain, and very little hay until tomorrow. Eugene's lethargic stance and low-hung head convince me he won't be interested in eating anytime soon.

The others, however, are a different story. Three groups of horses—Nellie and friends out front; two mares in one back pasture; and four geldings in the other back pasture—mill around their entry gates. Each has an internal alarm as precise as the one I use to rise at 4:00 every morning. The horses' afternoon alarms go off just before 6:00 p.m., and have thus already sounded.

Agitation builds as they try to coexist in close proximity with one another, each eager to be escorted back into the barn before the other. The daily ritual has come full circle, with the horses as excited to return to their stalls as they were to leave them earlier in the day.

Horses gathering into a tighter and tighter herd is not a good thing. When they decide to congregate in such a small place, biting and kicking one another is predictable. They simply refuse to queue up and wait patiently to return to the nightly comfort of their stalls.

Do I bring them into their stalls without available grain, or do I leave them to congregate at the gate? I ponder.

Each choice has its own distinct pitfall. If I bring them in without grain readily available, they'll move back and forth in their stalls, occasionally kick walls and doors, and periodically chew on available objects like their feeders and water buckets. If I leave them outside, there will still be kicking and biting, but it will be directed at one another. I opt to bring them inside, rationalizing that stall-repairing is preferable to horse-healing.

The only choice is to start with the mares in the front pasture, who are decidedly more impatient for dinner than the geldings in the side pasture. I enter the front pasture and retrieve Nellie. I shoo the other horses back a bit to avoid a conflict and to have space enough to place a halter over her head without fear of being kicked by one of the others. Even if I were willing to be fair about which horse gets to leave the field first, Nellie sees herself as queen and is least willing to give ground. Consequently, she's always closest to the gate.

Neither am I surprised at the order the others are removed: Star, then Prissy. The mares in the back pasture also have their social order. Pepper aggressively shoos Lacy away from the gate, forcing me to take her first. The removal pattern is based upon this social pecking order and is exactly the same every day.

After Lacy is safely in her stall, I decide to take a big chance on the geldings. Eugene is already in his stall and the mares are tucked safely away. I open wide the stall doors for Zach, Apollo, Mojito, and Macho Man. Then I make certain that the rear entry into the barn is unobstructed. When I return to the gelding pasture, I simply open the gate and let them out. They jostle a bit for position, then rapidly move through the open gate and trot down the drive toward the barn. Each finds its appropriate stall and heads straight to the feeder. Given that the feeders are empty, I hustle behind them to close the stall doors before they discover the ruse.

To my surprise, the horses are initially more patient than I'd imagined, though I'm sure this won't last long.

How about the neighbors? I wonder. Somebody must have sweet grain to spare on a Sunday afternoon in June. The neighbors to the east have sheep, the ones to the rear only a few chickens. Bud owns the only horse farm nearby and is just across the 10-acre corn field.

I fantasize that there's more than one potential neighbor to tap, but know there's only a single viable option.

Bud Reardon, at 76, knows more about horses than anyone in the county. If you don't believe it, just ask him. A self-proclaimed horse whisperer, he can, and will, tell you more than you ever wanted to know. While I appreciate his willingness to advise a newbie with a steep learning curve, his dogmatic and condescending approach has caused me to avoid him entirely.

I'm the laughingstock of our rural community, and no wonder. Bud's gone out of his way to tell anyone who'll listen how many times I've gotten my truck stuck down by the creek—four, to be exact. He's retold the unfortunate story of the horse that accidentally escaped my grasp and raced across the adjoining field—soy bean that year—crashing his daughter's garden wedding. As bad as we felt about the disrupted nuptials, he didn't have to keep retelling the story all over town.

Bud's advice is endless, and his style so annoying that I have a hard time being in the same room with the man.

Ironically, we chose the sweet grain we feed the horses based upon his adamant advice. I know full well that the ever-wise and ever-prepared Bud has a grain-shed full sweet grain. He'll be more than willing to share, but I know he'll probe and probe until I reveal Eugene's gorging and the resulting lack of grain for Sunday dinner. Then he'll add a new story to his list of my boneheaded, novice mistakes on the farm. Given how many times I've heard him repeat tales of my past goof-ups, maybe he could use some new material.

If my cell phone had power, I'd swallow what little pride I have left on this unfortunate day, and call Bud to ask for grain.

With no functioning phone, I'll have to head over to his farm and handle the request in person.

The quickest way in and out will be to use our little green ATV to drive right up to the front of his feed-shed: I can leave the ATV running, find Bud, and ask him politely to lend me some grain. Then, according to my plan, I'll throw a bag of grain from the shed onto the back rack and wheel off without having to offer an explanation or receive unwanted advice.

The direct route to Bud's farm is across the corn field, but the corn is already knee high and, even though we don't know well the farmer who leases the property, racing across the field would be another mess-up worthy of a Bud story.

I've seen the farmer himself regularly driving through the field with a similar ATV, but it's clear I don't have such rights.

Still, the ATV flies, and it won't take any time at all to traverse the back of our hay field, passing along the wooded property line to the back of Bud's place.

I take off along the hay field with both dogs racing alongside. I'm impressed that they keep up with the speedy ATV, running across uneven ground with only their heads visible as they bob through grass higher than their backs. I'm never certain whether they enjoy the run, or are just burdened by severe separation anxiety.

The hounds and I arrive at the far west boundary of our hay field where it borders the adjacent cornfield. I ease off the thumb throttle just enough to bear right. Then, through a quick acceleration, I dash through the shade of the walnut trees lining the property along the back edge of the 20-acre cornfield that separates Bud's property from ours.

I slow dramatically, take a hard right, and cross onto Bud's hay field. Unlike our thigh-high field, his field has been recently cut, and in this state resembles a lawn more suitable for croquet than a source of food for livestock. I travel slowly across his back-five acres, respecting his property and admiring the neatly manicured field.

Mad dashes always stimulate the dogs' digestive system. Neither can resist the short grass, and they both take the slowed pace as an opportunity to stop and defecate on Bud's hay field. Real farmers, especially tough old birds like Bud, shouldn't express concern about such an act of nature, but

I know it would bother him if he witnessed it or stumbled across the remnants. Perversely, I'm pleased at that prospect.

My ATV rolls up in front of the grain shed and I leave it running while I search the adjacent barn and outbuildings for Bud. There are no lights on anywhere. I presume the electricity is still out and that Bud is around somewhere. I exhaust the search out back and head toward the house. The garage door is up and the emergency cord has been pulled to release the door from its electric opener. Bud's pickup is gone. The single car garage is empty and I'm relatively sure Bud isn't home.

I press the ringer at the door leading into Bud's house from the garage and wait, but it's not long before I realize that doorbells don't work without electricity either. I knock gently but barely wait for a response.

"Must not be home," I mutter to myself as I turn quickly to exit the garage and race back to the ATV, recognizing his absence as a godsend.

The simple latch on his shed is meant to keep it shut, not secure from intruding neighbors. It opens easily. I enter the grain shed and find exactly what I expected. The 12' by 12' wooden shed is filled with stacks of 40-pound bags of sweet grain, the exact brand that we serve. There must be over 200 sacks of grain! Even Bud wouldn't be anal enough to count it daily, or keep an inventory of this much grain.

"He'll never miss one. Hell, he'll never miss a couple."

I've put two bags onto the ATV's back rack, strapping them down with bungee cords, before the dogs finish sniffing the inside of the shed, searching for spilled traces of molasses-coated oats. I quietly call them out, close and latch the shed door, and turn the ATV toward Bud's back hay field. Avoiding the strong temptation to escape quickly through the knee-high corn—the direct route—I retrace our entry path. The dogs are far out in front, making their way to the back corner of the property. The wooded back border is home to rabbits and other small critters which, they hope, will provide them an entertaining chase.

My brief sense of accomplishment from a well-executed larceny fades quickly as I wheel between the two piles of dog poop, one five feet to my right, the other a little farther out to the left. The piles lie innocently in a field that will be waist high in a few weeks. The hay bind will cut above them such that they'll never grossly impact Bud's bales. Nonetheless, I'm oddly ashamed at the sight.

The ATV rolls to a stop as I remove my thumb from the throttle and ponder the piles. The dogs hear the subtle change in engine tone, halt, and turn for visual cues to understand the unexpected turn of events. I imagine they've forgotten their role in the act that prompts my concern. Otherwise, they'd keep running.

I turn the ATV around and head back to Bud's barn. Stall picks, various-sized shovels, and push brooms hang neatly on the wall just inside the barn adjacent to his workbench. As I reach for a shovel, a bright yellow paper pad on the workbench inexplicably catches my attention.

"Damn!" I mutter, grabbing the pad along with the pencil

lying next to it, giving in to the inevitable.

I grudgingly scratch out a note and rip it angrily from the pad.

Bud, ran out of grain and needed to borrow a couple of bags. Hope that's OK? Will replace tomorrow.

—Adam C

I place the note in clear view in the grain shed, gather the shovel, and drive the ATV to the back field.

Both dog messes fit easily on the blade of the shovel, and a quick one-handed drive back to the property line allows me to fling the crap directly into the woods. Ironically, I don't know, or even care, who owns the woods.

Returning the shovel to the barn, I'm bothered by the recognition that I was prepared to steal the grain and leave the poop as a semi-secret confirmation of my presence. At the same time, I'm disgusted that I couldn't follow through with such a harmless transgression.

Sunday June 18, 1967

Sam sat tall in the pew, feigning interest in the homily. His left leg was strategically crossed over his right, with ankle resting on knee, so he could inconspicuously scratch his lower left shin through his dark sock.

"Stop scratching it!" I hissed under my breath. "They'll want to see it."

I sat in the pew next to my older, thirteen-year-old brother, knowing full well the source of his discomfort and why he couldn't stop scratching it. As his ever-present accomplice, I was experiencing a sympathy itch and felt tempted to scratch my own shin.

We were never crazy about going to church, and it was particularly difficult to gain spiritual motivation on this calm Sunday morning when the bayou would be slick as glass. It was Father's Day and, as egocentric children are prone to do, we had convinced Pop that taking his two sons water skiing with two of their friends would make his day. Undoubtedly, he could have thought of a dozen more leisurely ways to enjoy himself than driving a boat in circles with pre-teens screaming instructions from the end of a rope.

Just before heading to church, Sam and I had tried to eke out one more Sunday morning activity before having to don the dreaded tie, jacket, and socks. Still in our sleeping shorts, without shirt or shoes, we had quietly eased out through the carport door and into the "lab," which housed an introductory chemistry set I'd received a month earlier for my eleventh birthday. The set was proudly displayed on an old card table in the storage shed beside the garage, the periodic table of elements prominently displayed on top of the plastic box containing small, neatly arranged vials of chemicals. The table listed the 103 elements that had been discovered by 1966, 14 fewer than were in the table nearly 50 years later.

Sam and I had paid little attention to any of the basic lessons to be learned about the chemical elements. We had minimal interest in their elemental composition. Rather, we'd focused on the most visible and impressive effects of combining substances. We supplemented the chemical supply of charcoal and sulfur with saltpeter from the local pharmacy, a combination that created gunpowder which wouldn't quite explode, but generated enough smoke to greatly impress the younger boys in the neighborhood. We also discovered that combining vinegar and baking soda in your mouth created foam convincing enough to fool your mother into thinking you'd been poisoned. Most impressively, these scientific secrets were passed along to our pre-teen friends by word of mouth—there were no assists from a then non-existent Internet.

Only the Lord knows what type of experiment we were attempting when I bumped the very unstable card table and a splash of sulfuric acid landed on the front of Sam's shin, just above his ankle.

"Boys!" Pop called out the door leading from house to carport. "Get ready for church." The neutral call was neither questioning nor demanding, but the meaning was clear. We were expected to move quickly.

We rushed back into our room to throw on our Sunday best. As emerging Southern gentlemen from the gulf coast of northwest Florida, we wore our Top-Sider boat shoes to church with khakis, button-downed pastel dress shirt, tie, and blue blazer. In church, unlike every other setting in our beach town, socks were mandatory. We would later wear the same shoes with shorts and no shirt to traverse the unbearably hot asphalt before walking straight into the bayou to launch the ski boat. Sam hastily threw on the dreaded socks with no attempt to wipe the sulfuric acid from his shin.

In comparison with those of other religions, Episcopal services are relatively short. A pithy priest can get you in and out in thirty-five minutes, and Reverend Cobb was trying that Father's Day to be pithy. Nonetheless, the promise of water skiing, along with the acid eating a hole in one of Sam's only socks, made it feel as if we were condemned to the very eternity the sage priest was describing in his sermon.

As soon as the last stanza of the recessional ended, we uncharacteristically begged out of the social that always followed the service. Normally, we were anxious to shed the tie and socks, and eager to be rewarded for our patience with a couple of Krispy Kreme donuts, but getting to the car to remove Sam's sock trumped a donut this morning.

Fortunately, the substance labeled "sulfuric acid" in an amateur chemistry set must be considerably diluted. Sam lost a little skin when pulling off the sock, but with the attention to deception that only pre-teens can achieve, we were able to conceal the injury sufficiently to make sure we could follow through with our water-skiing plans. It would take considerable skill to hide a wound just above the top of the foot during an activity that requires bare feet, but we were confident in our ability to dissemble, and our feet would be underwater most of the day anyway.

Sam and I were fortunate enough to live almost on the water, across the street from a beautiful, peaceful bayou that emptied into the bay, which subsequently emptied into the Gulf of Mexico. We could see the bayou's glistening surface through the wooded lot that separated us from our favorite pastime.

Yet, there is a considerable difference between living on the water and living almost on the water. The real estate for the former is five times as expensive as the latter, perhaps because the water is five times as accessible. My parents would one day live directly on the water and have the luxury of keeping a boat in the water at all times. As is usually the case, the grandchildren—my children and Sam's—inspired this move and reaped the benefits.

Sam and I had to invest a lot more effort in our boat trips back then. We laboriously loaded the boat that day with the necessary equipment, used a trailer to bring it a half mile up the road, then jockeyed for position with ten other weekend boaters who cautiously, and often unsuccessfully, zigzagged their trailers down the narrow concrete ramp and into the water. After launching, we drove the truck and empty trailer back to the vacant lot across the street from our house. The duration of the entire exercise far exceeded morning worship time.

The wheels were barely settled in the driveway at home before Sam and I bolted from the car and into the house to change into the swimsuits we planned to wear until dark. Our 19-foot Thunderbird ski boat was loaded and we were fully prepared to head across the street for the morning launch when Mom summoned Pop inside for a phone call. Calls on

Sunday morning weren't common, but when one came, it was never just one.

"Crap," Sam muttered under his breath.

"No way," I whispered. We were all too aware of what this might mean for our plans.

Pop's name made the local newspaper every day; he was listed on the inside cover as publisher. He ascended to this rank with no college degree and no experience as a journalist. His dedication to and success in collecting debt from advertisers led to a better job selling advertising to the same deadbeats, which eventually led to running the advertising department, which kept the paper viable, at least according to the traditional newspaper business model of the day. His constant attention to the bottom line was apparent, and when the owners of the paper were faced with the choice between appointing a new leader based on editorial merits or on those related to profit and loss, he became the publisher.

Our home phone number was published in the paper every day next to Pop's name. Farther down the list of names and numbers, you could find the advertising department where he once worked, the circulation department with a number to call with delivery problems, and the stately editor whose name and scathing editorials were much better known in the small community but whose phone number was conspicuously absent. On the list of numbers for disgruntled customers, Pop's always appeared first.

Before cable news and well before the digital age, the morning paper was, for many, the lifeline to the world's happenings. Morning coffee simply wasn't consumed without a newspaper spread wide across the kitchen table. The paper was thrown onto the driveway from the bike of the most industrious kid in the neighborhood, and was immediately retrieved by an awaiting subscriber in robe and slippers.

If the delivery kid's mom forgot to wake him, the guy in the robe eventually marched back inside and called the first number he could find in the paper—our home number. If the press broke, the entire paper had to be distributed after all of the kids were in school, and the number of angry people needing their news-fix multiplied exponentially, causing our phone to ring off the hook.

Mom found it incredible that folks whose paper was late would call the publisher. Pop was simply disappointed that a customer was not pleased, and he felt compelled to personally rectify every failed delivery. The kid who delivered the paper to our home tossed half a dozen extras onto our driveway every day, and on weekdays, Pop fielded any early morning calls, retrieved the papers from the driveway in his suit, not robe, and weaved his way to the office disarming disgruntled customers with a personal delivery from the publisher. Most became Pop's most ardent supporters, but they still called him for their paper the next time it was late.

Weekday distribution mishaps were usually addressed while Sam and I were preparing for school, so we weren't overly aware of the impact on Pop's schedule. Weekends were a different story. When the phone rang, we knew our Sunday plans were about to change.

Pop emerged from the house as feared, in slacks and a casual but crisply ironed short-sleeve shirt. We checked to see if he had on the tell-tale socks to confirm our suspicion. Yep, socks! We weren't aware how many times the phone rang while he was inside changing clothes, but paid close attention to the number of papers under his arm. In this case, there were three.

Mom was at the door and nodded toward the car as she caught our disappointed gaze. We were being asked to accompany Pop on his delivery chores. It was Father's Day, and thus our duty as his children. The boat wouldn't be leaving the dock without him anyway, so we jumped into the car. It was already 10:30 a.m. We had opted for an 8:00 a.m. church service in order to have more time on the water, but now the day was quickly slipping away.

"Shotgun," I yelled as I squeezed past Sam into the front seat. He unceremoniously piled in right next to me, pushing me to the center of the bench seat, next to Pop. We drove 35 minutes north of town with no conversation and no radio for entertainment. Radios were optional in 1966, as was air-conditioning, and Pop apparently considered them both a luxury rather than a necessity. (It gets hot in northern Florida in June, and the air flow in the Dodge Rambler at 45 mph doesn't compare to a Thunderbird ski boat at half the speed. Somehow, while we sat sweating in silence, Pop appeared cool and dry.)

We finally pulled off the winding country road we'd been following since leaving town and onto a short gravel driveway leading to a small wooden house with peeling white paint and sporadic but overgrown shrubs. The Rambler came to a stop in the dusty drive behind a 1959 Ford pickup truck complete with an empty gun rack, a National Rifle Association sticker on one side of the back bumper, and a "Jesus Saves" sticker on the other.

"Wait here." Pop uttered the first two words of the trip as he picked up one of the papers, opened the car door, and headed for the house.

Sam and I waited as he approached the front door. There was nothing particularly menacing about the place. Pickup trucks with gun racks were common in those parts. The NRA sticker signaled an ultra-conservative, but not necessarily violent, citizen of the South. Nonetheless, my heart quickened a bit as Pop strode toward the door. Sam looked concerned as well.

Before Pop could get a foot onto the small concrete pad serving as a front porch, the door flew open and a large older man stepped forward, forcefully blocking Pop's way. He led with a big belly and a dirty white t-shirt, stopping just short of using it to force Pop off of the step leading up onto the pad. Pop kept one foot on the step and the other firmly planted on the ground.

The man's tattered camouflage pants couldn't contain his belly, which had settled into a less strained position close to his crotch. The gray hair on his exposed belly was thick and impressive compared to the relatively few long and wispy strands that remained on his age-spotted head. His oversized forearms were the only clue that a previous life of labor might have kept him in slightly better shape during his younger years.

"That gosh-darned fish wrapper of yours ain't worth wastin' good pulp wood to make," he growled when he saw the paper tucked under Pop's arm. Old newspapers were routinely used to wrap fish at the local market, and pulp wood wasn't exactly an exotic hard wood. It was the harshest complaint the man could muster.

Sam and I continued watching and listening intently from the Rambler. Even at our age, we were puzzled. Why had we come all this way to deliver a paper to a disgruntled man clearly anxious to receive it, even as he claimed to despise its contents?

Pop tried to slide the paper forward from under his arm without brushing up against the man's exposed belly. He extended the weighty, advertisement-filled Sunday paper, which stretched the limits of its original rubber band, to the waiting customer.

"I'm Wade," he said calmly. "Wade Cherry, the publisher of this fish wrapper," he added with a gentle smile.

The man opened his mouth to unleash a second round of obscenities, then froze, realizing what he had heard. He stepped back quickly, putting a more appropriate space between Pop and his belly.

"You're who? You're what?"

"The publisher, Wade Cherry," Pop repeated, nodding his head slowly and continuing to smile as the man looked him up and down, trying to sort through the unexpected information.

The man instinctively took the paper from Pop, held it by his side, and continued to gaze at the individual on his porch. "You drove all the way from town just to deliver this paper to me?" he asked softly, gesturing toward the paper with his free hand before lifting it to brush back a swath of hair that no longer existed.

Pop's nodding and smiling continued.

The man switched his hand from the hair on his head to that on his exposed belly as he pondered this strange turn of events. Suddenly realizing the inappropriateness of his earlier response, he put the paper under his left arm so he could use both hands, one to stretch his t-shirt down, the other to hoist up his trousers by lifting the front of his low-slung belt. The attempt to cover himself was clearly motivated by respect for Pop's position and a sudden appreciation for the extraordinary customer service.

Sam and I sat in the car observing the encounter and counting the minutes. We exhaled when Pop turned down the man's offer to come inside and share a morning beer. We grimaced when he remained on the porch receiving specific, yet much more respectful, feedback on the skills and biases of various journalists on the newspaper staff and the insufficient coverage of Crimson Tide football.

Fourteen minutes into the conversation, I reached over and gently placed my hand on the car horn, shooting a questioning glance at Sam. He quickly lunged across my body to yank my hand from the horn and simultaneously deliver a short-armed punch into my rib cage.

"You idiot!" he whispered angrily, knowing Pop was still within earshot of the open car windows.

Pop graciously waited for an opening to return to the car, which did not come until thirty-four minutes after we'd pulled into the dusty drive. Sam and I watched quietly, unwilling to disrupt the conversation. Any attempt to stand between Pop and his duty would clearly jeopardize our water-skiing trip.

Similar scenes played out on two more porches over the next hour and eight minutes. Neither was as dramatic as Mr. Borden's, but both ended with the same level of undisputed customer satisfaction.

After that day, Mr. Borden called the newspaper often, always asking to speak to his new friend, "Publisher Cherry." Pop wasn't in the habit of reporting daily work events to Sam and me, but he related Mr. Borden's most recent complaint or compliment each time he called. Perhaps he was checking to see if we noticed that the complaints were fewer and less vitriolic, and the compliments more frequent and profuse. We noticed.

We made it home that day in time to hook up the trailer and pull the boat down the street to the boat ramp. Pop scooted the white Thunderbird across the quarter-mile wide bayou to pick up two of our friends, and we had the first skier up and slaloming by 2:00 p.m.

Pop, or "Ski-Daddy" as our friends called him, wasn't a big skier, but he welcomed the opportunity to drive the boat. Aptly named, Ski Daddy would pull us behind the boat as long as we had ample gas, daylight, and boys with arms strong enough to hold the rope. Pop's greatest joy came from watching us have fun.

We took turns skiing all afternoon. We'd ski alone, then put out a second rope and ski in pairs. Sam even tried to step out of a ski to "barefoot," but his vicious falls made Pop grimace and eventually he gave Sam a thumb's down as we swung around to pick him up after yet another failed attempt.

The gas gauge dipped below the halfway mark as the sun touched the horizon at water's edge. Pop, ever cautious, headed to the marina for a fill-up before dark. Our arm strength ran lower than the gas and fading daylight. With a full tank, we headed through the early evening calm toward the boat launch, content to call it a day.

By the time we made it back to the ramp, unloaded the boat, and pulled it the short distance back to the house, it was completely dark. Father's Day was winding down. Nonetheless, Pop was unwavering in his boat-cleaning ritual, which he regarded as yet another duty. It would be a full hour before we would head inside to clean ourselves.

We washed the boat, pumped fresh water through the foot of the motor, and made certain to put the skis and life vests in their appointed positions in the shed. Together, we hoisted the customized canvas cover over the entire craft and tied it into place. When we shut down the spotlight that had illuminated our work and headed indoors, the boat was fully prepared for its next voyage.

Pop had spent his entire Father's Day in service to his work and his children. At breakfast, just before the acid incident, he'd opened a card and a present. That was the extent of official Father's Day activities. Sam and I had at least signed the card (after three reminders from Mom), but were clueless about the wrapped contents. We watched curiously as he opened the present to find a new pair of work gloves.

"Just what I wanted," he proclaimed without a hint of sarcasm.

"Glad you like them," I said. Sam shamelessly added, "We thought you would."

Pop was driven by duty: to meet the needs of his family, and to do the right thing as well as he knew how. His commitment to this broad sense of duty appeared to be driven purely by internal motivation. No audience was needed, no awards were necessary. If he was convinced a task was his duty, he completed it.

Mom once persuaded him that it was his fatherly duty to give the "sex talk" to Sam and me. Unfortunately, this was when we were a bit too young for the lecture; Sam was about to turn eight years old and I was only six. Pop, ever diligent and prepared to fulfill his duty, summoned us to the living room just after dinner one evening.

"Boys, I have something to talk to you about," he began.

We were all ears. Pop usually had very little to say, and when he did talk, it was brief. This time, he appeared to be settling in for what might be a longer conversation.

"What did we do?" I asked, assuming that the only reason

he would sit us down for a long chat was to correct a misdeed of some kind.

"Don't worry," he said. "I just need to tell you where babies come from."

Now he had our full attention. For the next fifteen minutes, we sat on the edge of our seats as Pop used the appropriate medical terminology to describe male and female body parts, and continued with a technical explanation of "coitus" complete with a hand gesture which included a forefinger on one hand and a hole created with the other forefinger and opposing thumb. The hand gesture was the least technical and most unprofessional part of his explanation.

Sam sat transfixed but scowling. Lost by the technical terms, I fidgeted, but sensed the awkwardness enough to not ask questions. As Pop completed his explanation, Sam found that he could no longer contain his disgust.

"Ewwwwwww!" he shrieked. "That means you and Mom had to do that twice!"

Effective or not, Pop had fulfilled his paternal duty.

In 1964, well before most fathers were openly engaged in the school lives of their children, Pop was elected president of our elementary school's Parent Teacher Association. Other parents at the meeting, mostly mothers, weren't willing to assume the leadership. He was reluctant, but willing to do his duty. He was re-elected, uncontested, for two consecutive terms.

Six years later, when Sam and I were bussed to Booker T. Washington High School, Pop took a very public stand in favor of desegregation. While most of our friends from all-white suburbs went to newly created private schools, Pop insisted that it was his duty to make sure that we attended our designated public school, the previously all-black Booker T.

He and a biracial group of parents started the first booster club at the school and raised thousands of dollars for previously non-existent extracurricular programs. They fought for fair funding, better instruction, and an integrated voice for parents. Well over a decade later, the old dilapidated school was replaced with a brand new facility and became a model for the state of Florida.

"Where babies come from" was Pop's sole lecture. He never sat us down for the "Do the right thing" lecture.

It wasn't necessary.

INFLUENCE

CHAPTER EIGHT

Happy horses greet me when I return with their grain. They wait, though not all of them patiently, for me to distribute food and supplements into their buckets.

Eugene scrapes the floor repeatedly with his left front hoof, begging for grain as I approach his stall. When it's clear I'm passing him by, he violently kicks the side of the stall wall, startles me, and causes a handful of grain to spill from the feed bucket. This delights the dogs, who always observe the feeding ritual closely for just such a mishap.

As the herd munches grain, I climb the steps into the loft above their stalls to drop hay and to feed the barn cats a scoop of dry food—not too much, I make sure, lest the cats lose their motivation to "mouse." Square bales of hay, inappropriately named given that they're rectangles, are stacked from floor to ceiling in the 20-foot loft above the stalls. I know the stacks well, having harvested each bale from the back field under late summer's harsh sun last year. Each was stacked on the hay wagon as it came out of the baler, then strategically restacked above each horse's stall after riding the hay elevator from the wagon to the loft.

Above each horse's stall is an eighteen-inch-square opening in the hay loft floor. The openings allow one to drop flakes of hay directly into a heavy, wrought-iron rack mounted on a side wall in the stall. The rack catches the hay to keep it from falling to the stall floor and mixing with urine or manure. The hay bales are stacked close to each hole, and "dropping hay flakes," as horse folks call it, is among the easiest of evening chores.

I drop two to four flakes into each stall, depending upon the age and size of the horse, or the owner's informed notion of what constitutes the perfect diet. Though each flake comes off the bale at slightly different widths, the thickness averages three inches, and a typical bale contains a dozen or more flakes. This evening, Eugene gets one small flake to tide him over until breakfast.

Nonetheless, by the time I've delivered grain, supplements, and hay, then filled all ten water buckets, it's after 8:00. The summer sun is dropping toward the horizon, but it won't slip completely over the tree tops this time of year until nearly nine.

My makeshift sustenance from beer and chips has totally faded. Suddenly famished, I finally contemplate dinner. Fresh caught fish is the plan, but the power's still out. All of the electric appliances in the house are useless. I was convinced of the need for a generator after our first storm-caused outage on the farm, but as always, I procrastinated. The Weber grill should be an option, but charcoal is about as available as horse grain. I'm certainly not inclined to return to Bud's place for that.

Why am I never prepared? I think, disappointed in myself once again.

The homemade fire pit next to the pond appears to be the only option. It's nothing more than some random rocks collected from the pastures and stacked atop one another, three high, encircling an area the size of the galvanized trash can lid Eugene removed earlier this morning. But the fire it can bind is more than enough for cooking a single fish. Besides, it's the perfect opportunity to try out the new bench, strategically positioned behind the pit and facing the water. Perhaps I've created a serene spot for an evening campfire.

Since we moved to the farm, I've been removing old and broken fence rails, cutting them into firewood length and stacking them against the shed. The thin, aged wood burns fast and hot. Not wanting the smell of diesel fuel or lighter fluid to taint the flavor of my hard-caught fish, I decide to build a fire the old-fashioned way. A match lights the side of a mound of dry hay the size of a bird's nest. The hay ignites small dry twigs as they're added. Little twigs light larger ones placed strategically over the growing blaze. The twigs give way to small pine branches, which are almost subsumed by slightly larger birch limbs, until the fire is ready for the old fence rails. Twenty minutes later, seven pieces of fence rail have produced a perfect pile of hot embers.

Despite the lack of electricity, the garage fridge stayed cold enough to keep the fish from spoiling, as I had predicted. I retrieve the whole fish with one hand and grab a half-filled bottle of chardonnay in the other and set them on the edge of the new bench, I take a small Swiss Army knife from my jeans pocket, unfold the small but sturdy blade, and approach the apple tree a few yards from the pond. An ideally sized and shaped branch is at eye level. I cut it from the tree with three hard swipes and unceremoniously strip its leaves clean.

After sharpening one end of the branch to a lethal point, I skewer the fish, running the limb from its tail into the flesh along its backbone, through its head, and straight out of its mouth. The weight of the fish on the thin, green limb bends it toward the embers, like a divining rod to water, when I hold it over the fire. Nonetheless, the branch provides sufficient stability to rotate the fish and continually reposition it above the fire, so all parts cook.

Being closest to the embers, the fish head catches fire twice. Each time I pull it from the fire, I wave my free hand furiously and blow with fully extended jowls until I'm feeling lightheaded. The strategy extinguishes the blaze, but not before the fish face is completely charred. The flesh should still be perfect, but the burned-out eyes on the dull ashen head create a disturbing effect that many would find unappetizing.

I sit on the bench and hold the fish upright, proudly and carefully inspecting it while waiting for it to cool. No table, no utensils, no bread, no salad, no salt, no pepper, and no glass. But I do have wine. I grab the chardonnay bottle off of the adjacent trunk stool, yank the cork out with my front teeth, and spit it over the fire and into the pond like a pirate. Remembering the afternoon beer fiasco, I take less than a pirate-like swig.

The fish cools in minutes. I return the wine bottle to the bench and, with a refined pincer grasp, gently pull a chunk of meat from the section of the bass just above the tail but short of the rib cage. I understand Pisces anatomy enough to know that the pinch won't result in a bite full of tiny bones. The thin skin and well-cooked meat underneath easily pulls off in a large chunk.

It could be that I'm so damn hungry. It could be that the fish is so fresh. It could be the pure ambiance of the evening. Whatever the reason, the flavor is priceless!

I successfully avoid imagining the health-related issues associated with a fish raised in a small farm pond that receives periodic chemical treatments for overabundant algae and is inevitably exposed to some level of toxic runoff from the adjacent, well-fertilized corn field. Were Betty around, she would be certain to remind me. I choose to focus on the fish and its beneficial effect on my appetite.

I pick at the fish from every angle, stopping only for a short sip from the open bottle. Occasionally, I switch the skewer-holding hand with the fish-picking hand. Each switch provides a better angle and reveals a section of the fish not yet stripped clean. I'm careful around the bones of the rib cage, but otherwise move quickly to devour the crispy skin and succulent meat. In a matter of minutes, the charred head sits atop a hanging backbone, with rib cages on either side fully attached.

Seeing the tail still intact and a good bit of solid meat around its base, I return to the fire and thrust the carcass to within an inch of the blazing red embers. In seconds, the tail fully ignites. I immediately pull it from the fire and use my now-refined waving-and-blowing technique to extinguish it. Removing the entire tail section from the larger carcass, I carefully nibble off crispy pieces of the fanned-out fish tail, the *coup de grâce* of barbecued delight.

I've successfully paced myself with the wine, and plenty remains in the bottle. *No more gun-shooting sprees tonight.* Long shadows creep across the pond and I peer west in time to see the bright orange ball drop below the fence-line of trees as the field begins to darken.

Stuffed with fish and mellowed by wine, I sit hypnotized by the fire as the tranquil twilight fades to darkness. The few frogs who've eluded the snake are croaking sporadically as crickets rub their legs with more rhythmic and regular tones. The setting begs for one more vice—a cigar.

The humidor is only yards away, having been moved into the storage shed for just such an occasion. Why store cigars inside when I only smoke them outside? Besides, the humid summer air keeps them in better shape than any of the air-conditioned storage options.

I walk inside the shed and retrieve a smuggled Cohiba, but don't bother to retrieve a match or a cutter to snip the end. Such accessories wouldn't fit the rustic nature of the evening any more than a wire coat hanger would have sufficed as a fish skewer. Taking the cigar from its cellophane enclosure, I bite the tip off of the torpedo end and spit a tiny chunk of tobacco into the grass as I walk back to the fire.

The unlit end of one of the smaller limbs used to start the fire sticks out far enough for me to grab it without singeing the hair off the back of my hand. As expected, the other end is red hot and perfect for lighting.

After four deep draws on the bitten-off end, a small blaze of burning tobacco momentarily erupts. As soon as I stop puffing, the blaze subsides and casts a plume of light gray smoke toward the pond. I inspect the lit end to assure it won't need a few more tokes before tossing the limb back into the fire. Satisfied, I return to the new bench to relax and enjoy.

I like the act of smoking a cigar, but am not entirely convinced that I like cigars themselves. I don't smoke many, but when I do, it's to cap something off—a celebration, a wake, the successful delivery of a child, a hard-fought win, a sealed deal. As a behaviorist, I assume it's the paired association with these capstone experiences that maintains my pleasure in the occasional vice. I've never smoked cigarettes, and I fully understand that the health risks of cigars are as bad or worse, but I still gravitate to a stogie when the time is right.

Sitting on my new bench at a pond-side fire smoking a hand-rolled Cuban begs for reflection. I'd looked forward to this day for weeks. Now it's nearly over. Where did the time go and why? I'm not certain whether I'm smoking in celebration or in sorrow.

"Of all the days for the dog to take on a skunk," I say, beginning a litany of the day's grievances. "What're the chances that Eugene makes his escape on this specific day? The old manure spreader was bound to break sometime, but why today? No grain? We never run out of grain! And Nellie? Even you?"

Finally, "And that damn snake!"

I stare dejectedly at the ground in front of the bench for several minutes. Finally pulling myself from this moment of despair, I look into the night sky and realize that while I've been busy lighting cigars and inspecting the ground by my shoes, the stars have majestically populated the heavens. They look down on me by the thousands.

As I ponder the day's perils, it's hard to imagine that those who shaped it aren't watching. I fantasize that they're together, hooting with laughter, slapping one another on the back, staring from far above into the same little fire, cherishing the opportunity to recount my every move.

"A douche to clean a dog?" Granddaddy declares with a cock of his head and a big toothless smile. "Where the hell'd he come up with that?" He, more than anybody, revels in the creativity.

"Glad he got back on that nag!" Mal adds with no concern about the arrogance of suddenly changing the topic. "I knew he'd make it work with one more try. Just have to get back in the saddle, as they say." The others nod in total agreement.

Earl grins from ear to ear. "Caught that big ol' fish!" he exclaims, his hands stretched far apart to exaggerate its size like any respectable fisherman. "Then went right ahead and ate it—could smell it and almost taste it all the way up here. Sure am glad he didn't see the one that got away. Would've broken his heart. Biggest darn fish I've seen in a while. No matter, though. All turned out great. No harm done by a little tangled and broken line." His joy in retelling fish stories is apparent, but the others know his true delight is in the positive recasting of less than glorious deeds.

Pat's initial focus is the bench. "Sure would love to sit with him on that bench," he says longingly, then adds, "I knew he wouldn't let the small stuff get in the way. He really should think about digging a bigger pond, and maybe building just a little log cabin on its edge. Also, a rocker on the porch overlooking the new pond would be perfect for nights like this."

Coach Thomas hangs back a bit, but can't resist chiming in thoughtfully. "Glad Eugene's no worse for the wear. Sometimes it just takes time, a little tenderness, and a lot of cooling off."

Suddenly, they all fall silent and lower their gaze, simultaneously remembering the drunken snake-hunt. They stand motionless. Everyone but Earl expresses clear disappointment in my choices. True to form, he's never disappointed. Together, they take a moment to silently lament Grandpa Bob's absence from their heavenly circle of pride. Pop stands to the side, transfixed, as each makes their way to him and offers him a pat on the back, a gentle squeeze of the shoulder, or just a knowing glance.

Pop's stare into the fire below lingers until he unexpectedly breaks the silence with a jovial declaration: "I was most worried about the dog poop."

They burst into boyish laughter. *Timeless bathroom humor for men of all ages.*

"That would have been easy to overlook," he added. "But

when he turned that ATV around, I knew our work was done."

They all nod in agreement and return their loving gaze to earth.

Grandpa Bob died alone of liver failure in a senior citizens' home before I graduated from high school.

Granddaddy and Earl lost their respective fights with cancer in 1982.

Despite his careful diet, daily exercise, and self-proclaimed "top shape," Mal's heart let him down in 1986.

A few years later, Coach Thomas was caught in the crossfire of a drive-by shooting.

In his later years, Pat fell on his property, striking his head on a rock while staking out his final vision of an award-winning vineyard. He died on the hill above his beloved orchard.

Pop was with us until early this last spring. Cancer took him, just like it did Granddaddy and Earl.

They slipped away ever so slowly over the past few decades—so slowly that their powerful influence didn't sink in until they were gone.

I made it to some of their funerals, but not all. Needless to say, waiting until their burial didn't afford me the best opportunity to express my appreciation for their influence. I never took the time to thank them, or to directly acknowledge their extraordinary impact on my life. For years, I've harbored the guilt of those missed opportunities.

Under the stars at the edge of the pond, staring into the

fire with a shrinking cigar, tears leave tracks down my dusty cheeks. My day to piddle escaped as elusively as the chance to thank those men who'd shaped me.

Perhaps with their heavenly guidance, I'm struck by a new awareness. With the exception of Pop's failed sex education lecture, none of these extraordinary men ever sat me down to communicate their worldly lessons. Rather, the lessons were conveyed during moment-to-moment interactions. Likewise, I'd never stated out loud my sincere acknowledgement for the role they'd played in my life, only conveyed it in the way I approached the daily challenges of life.

The cigar, now the size of a wine cork, burns brightly and closer to my fingers. I rarely smoke more than an inch or two, but fantasy and contemplation have drawn this one down to a nub. I flip what's left into the embers of the dying campfire and sit a few minutes longer, enjoying the near-summer's eve.

Bo snoozes in the grass next to me. For the first time all day, I'm convinced I don't need to sniff him for foul odor.

Eugene, familiarly extended out of his stall window, is craning his neck to see what's prompted me to stay out this late by the pond. He finished his tiny flake of hay before the others. The rest still munch leisurely.

I look down at the bench and can't help but bounce a bit, testing and admiring its secure and sturdy build. I run my index finger around and around the grooves of the circle encompassing the "BC." This will be the first night of many that the bench serves us well. Maybe I'll build more. Maybe I'll personalize each, one for every member of the family. Pat, if no one else, would appreciate that.

Tomorrow, after work, I'll saddle Nellie and ride her about in the arena with no tolerance for messing around. I'm half-certain she'll comply, but only half. I rise a bit, stretching a sore back and rubbing the thighs of jeans still covered in arena dust; both reminders of my slow-motion flip into the sand. Skipping over the part where I'm lying flat on the arena floor, with Nellie looming over me, I picture her crisp turn and quick halt, all at my mounted command.

"I rode my Nellie today," I say out loud with pride and some disbelief. Lola and Bo look up from their slumber to make certain the enthusiastic statement isn't somehow tied to a celebration involving food. Seeing none, they reclose their eyes.

The gun? Did I really shoot it? I ponder the question with much less passion. *That's just crazy!*

Though my day yielded no prize snake to show off to Betty, I had secretly wanted to try that gun for a long time. Liquid courage prompted the ill-advised snake hunt, but I discovered the gun would fire and could be valuable, if only I could find appropriate and functional bullets.

There's plenty of grain for tomorrow morning's feeding, and that will make Betty happy. Bud'll be happy too, finding the note and adding a new episode to his collection of stories about the city boy run amuck on the horse farm.

Through good, bad, and pure ugly, I've piddled the day away. It was a "take it as it comes" kind of day, and it came and went. In hindsight, I've spent it just the way I planned.

My silent contemplation is interrupted by the loud whir of the air-conditioner fan restarting just outside the kitchen window. Lights from the house suddenly cast new and dramatic shadows on the dark pond and surrounding grounds. The hounds rise up to their paws and immediately head toward the house.

The area around the fire pit is free of grass and other flammables. I make certain the remaining fence-rail pieces are contained in the pit and that the fuel they've provided is almost depleted before following the dogs toward the garage. Were others here, I'd certainly be asked to douse the fire with water. Tonight, I'll take the very slight risk.

Lola and Bo wait patiently at the back door while I remove my boots, jeans, shirt, and socks, in that order. I take the dead cell-phone from my jeans pocket before piling the filthy clothes beside the door. I'll deal with them later. Wearing only briefs, I open the door and head into the kitchen, directly to the phone charger, which is already plugged into the wall. Gun shy in more ways than one, I decide that anything I touch with hand or body will end up on the front porch along with the soiled sofa. I vow that the next thing I touch will be the shower's faucet.

I stand patiently in front of the vanity mirror, waiting for the cold water in the old farm pipes to be replaced by hot water from the oversized tank we recently installed in the basement. My face is various shades of brown and black, with tear streaks still evident. I raise my chin high and look down my nose into the mirror, and spot a distinct ring of arena dirt filling a skin crease where my growing double chin meets my neck. As Granddaddy would have said: "Boy, there's enough dirt there to plant corn."

In a day filled with wild and strong sensations, the hot water cascading over my head is far and away the strongest. I stand under the water, bracing myself with both palms flush against the shower tile. It's a full five minutes before I make any effort to reach for soap or cloth. As the hydrotherapy relaxes the muscles in my back, I twist slightly at the waist, pleased with my improved ease of movement. Finally, I soap a wash cloth and engage in a more industrious effort to remove the day's dirt and grime.

The soft towel feels almost as good drying my back as the water did wetting it. Now dry, I wrap the towel around my waist and head out of the bathroom and across the master bedroom to fetch a much-needed and well-deserved pair of clean underwear. I open the drawer and am surprised to find three envelopes on top of my neatly folded and stacked tighty-whities.

The top envelope is white with the letters "A.C." handwritten on the outside: my initials and nothing else. The second envelope is the same size as the first, but yellow, and bears a postmark from Haiti. The final brown envelope is slightly larger than the others. It's addressed to Mr. Adam Cherry and bears a Los Angeles postmark.

I should have known. My wife and children know my routines so well, and would have predicted an early morning shower.

Guessing the intent of the card givers, I decide to open them in the order they were stacked. Standing in front of the dresser, still naked, I open the top envelope first. As expected, it's from Betty. The front of the card is a cartoon depiction of a man holding hands with two children sporting a large first-place blue ribbon on his chest labeled "Best Dad!" The inside has a similar photo of the same man, but the children have been replaced by a happy, attractive woman now holding his hand. An even larger ribbon with "Best Husband, Too!" is hung on his chest. Cute and flattering, the card includes a simple inscription: "Love you and miss you!—Betty."

The origins of the other two cards are obvious, so I decide to pull on a pair of underwear from the open drawer, adding my favorite sleeping shorts and the softest t-shirt in the dresser. It doesn't seem appropriate to open your children's Father's Day cards while still in the buff.

Fatigue catches me as I bend over to hoist up my shorts. I'm pooped, and my back is already losing the benefit of the hot shower. It's past time to close up shop and finally put this day to bed.

The dogs have already made this same decision and are curled up on their beds in their respective corners of the family room. They don't seem to miss the couch that still sits on the front porch. It'll be tomorrow's chore.

I head down to the kitchen and notice the phone has returned to life. It's muted, so I haven't heard the familiar but obnoxious antique car horn that announces incoming calls, texts, and e-mails. Family members and colleagues alike chastise me for having a phone that's always out of juice, silenced, or emitting ridiculous noises that I largely ignore. "Why even have a phone?" they ask.

The phone's been dead since mid-morning on a day when many would expect to reach me. Now, I hate to even glance at the screen. When I finally summon the nerve, eleven alerts stare back—five missed calls, three missed text messages, and three missed voice mails. As expected, the first call and accompanying voicemail of the day are from Betty.

"Hi, babe! Happy Father's Day!" she exclaims in a cheery voice, in contradiction of her usual disdain for early morning enthusiasm. "You must be in the shower! Call me when you're out and dressed." Had I heard this early morning clue, I'd have headed straight to the top dresser drawer.

Betty followed up her early morning greeting with a mid-morning call without leaving a message, but quickly switched to text with her typical brevity: "Out back?"

I try not to think about the fact that she called while I was out running water on Eugene's hooves without her knowledge. The phone registers her final attempt at 6:00 p.m. Her terse voicemail: "Hey, I'm really worried. What's up?"

A simple text has also arrived from both kids—"Happy Father's Day"—as has a missed call and solemn voice message from my aging mother, "Miss you and your dad on Father's Day. I know you're busy. No need to call back." Finally, a missed call and message at 9:10 p.m. from my youngest: "Happy Father's Day—AGAIN! It must have been busy. Hope it was fun. You're probably in bed by now. Talk to you tomorrow."

I immediately begin thinking about time zones, excuses, which daily stories to share, which to never share, whom to call first, who can really wait—this late and this exhausted, the chances of miscommunication are great. I allow myself more time to sort through the choices and decide to take the partially charged phone upstairs and to return the calls from the comfort of the bedroom.

I take one last peek out of the kitchen window into the star-lit night; first to confirm Eugene is still in his stall, second to assure myself that the decision to let the fire burn itself out isn't my last, and worst, of the day. Eugene surveys the evening landscape, his head protruding from the stall window. If he plans to try another escape, it'll be in the early morning hours tomorrow, and he'll be sorely disappointed by the security of an extra clip on the door.

A faint glow is visible in the fire pit, but I'm convinced that any popping ember would quickly burn out in the damp surrounding grass.

Satisfied with the external conditions, I turn off the downstairs lights and head upstairs. The bedroom lamp in the corner invites me to my favorite leather chair. The chair and its matching ottoman are usually covered with clothes—mine, Betty's, or some combination. Not necessarily dirty clothes, but ones that can be worn again, and don't quite deserve a place back in the drawers or closet with the totally clean ones.

Tonight, the chair is empty except for the hand-knit

olive-green afghan from my mother that's carefully folded and draped across its back. Betty always makes certain that the chair is clear before she leaves town, and I assume it was especially important for her that I have my "chair and blankie" unobstructed and available on this day.

I plop into the chair and exhale dramatically, over-emphasizing both my exhaustion and my comfort. I place the two unopened cards and the phone on the soft padded arms of the chair while reaching behind for the afghan. One big shake and it floats softly over my bare legs. I wiggle my bottom slightly in a not so masculine way and reach for the cards.

The yellow card sent all the way from Haiti is sealed with extra heavy tape, clearly applied by an anxious employee in the post office of that struggling country. It takes a bit more effort to open. When I'm finally able to extract the card, I feel a broad smile spread across my face and a light in my tired eyes. The front depicts a dad at a desk paying a large stack of bills. The top bill is from a university.

Four small pictures surround the larger one, each showing a kid learning something from a dad: helping with homework, throwing a ball, tying shoes, and driving a car. A close inspection reveals a globe sitting on the corner of the dad's desk. The inside is blank except for a line across the top which reads, "Thanks, Dad, for a world-class education!"

A handwritten note begins on the left side of the card, continues on the top right side under the text, and extends to the very bottom, the letters getting smaller as the space gets tighter.

Dad,

Sorry I missed Father's Day! Wish I could have been there. Better yet, wish you were here! We're working so hard to rebuild this little town and could use your help. The resilience of the people and their determination to start all over and persevere are so inspiring. Reminds me of our trip to Nicaragua where the kids had to walk so many miles to school and were still so eager to learn.

Not all of us agree about rebuilding in such squalor. Every day, I hope we're doing the right thing. As you might guess, I don't hide how I feel about it, but lucky for you, they haven't sent me home . . . yet. So many kids here are homeless and without parents. Makes me want to build an orphanage high on the beautiful hill above this mess. Want to help? I'm serious!

Come see me, please!

Love,

Jordy

I read the note twice, picturing this twenty-five-year-old graduate student spending the summer on that Third World island. The enthusiasm is contagious, the commitment inspiring. Worry over the well-being of a child so far away is overshadowed by pride. A warmth as soothing as the shower water consumes me.

I move to the final card, the brown one from Los Angeles. The front depicts multiple photos of kids of different ages obviously "in trouble" for various misdeeds. A preschool child has colored on the wall, an older child is looking at a report card with a failing grade, and an intoxicated teenager holds a beer. The tag-line on the outside reads, "Dad, remember all the trouble I caused you as a kid?"

The inside reads, "I'm almost done!"

This time, the typewritten note is on a separate page folded into fourths and inserted inside the card.

Dear Dad,

Too bad you're alone on Father's Day. Bummer! What will you do? All day by yourself. Please don't mope around all day doing chores. I actually picture a very pleasant day.

Thanks for understanding how busy I am. The new business is a blast. I sold two paintings yesterday. Two in one day! Nothing close to my old corporate money, but I'm getting by and find myself so excited when a stranger likes my work.

I know you like my stuff, but you have to. People actually pay real money for my creativity. Can you believe it? Besides, I don't have to put up with the folks at the office—they could be such a drag. I'm glad I finally found the backbone to take a stand and make a move.

Just wanted you to know that I'm so happy!

I know Mom hated to be on the road on Father's Day, even though you're not nearly old enough to be her dad!

Love you,

Chris

P.S. Sixty-four days clean and sober. One more after today.

No pressure!

Like the letter from Jordy, I reread this one carefully. Then back to read Jordy's letter once again. Then again to Chris'. After a few iterations of this process, I take another look at Betty's note and am fully satisfied.

I glance at the digital clock across the room, just as I did before the sun rose. It seems so long ago. The numbers read 10:12, not much past my typically early bedtime. Four a.m. isn't far away and there's much to do tomorrow. No time to piddle then.

Foregoing the effort involved in traversing the three feet from chair to bed, removing the large colorful throw pillows, and pulling back the covers, I simply pull the afghan up under my armpits, as high as it will go without uncovering my bare feet. One hand still holds the precious cards against my chest, while the other reaches for the switch on the floor lamp.

As soon as the room goes dark, the obnoxious antique car horn goes off on the phone, lighting up the chair arm next to me. It's a text from Betty.

"Night!"

I ponder the day's unspoken messages as I pick up the phone and search the illuminated keyboard.

"Night!" is my single-word reply.

Top Ten Ways to Honor Your Mentors

10. Relish the special times.

Take time to remember the special times you shared with your mentors. Reflect upon the lessons learned and relish the role they continue to play in shaping your life choices.

9. Appreciate your good fortune.

Recognize that not all children and youth have positive male role models. Count your blessings and be appreciative of the time you shared with your mentors.

8. Keep in touch.

Find ways to keep your mentors involved in your life. As we mature into adulthood, it's easy to lose touch with those who have had a profound impact on your life. Try hard to stay in touch. Reach out on their birthdays or on holidays, or find a special day tied to a unique event in your shared life.

7. Reconnect.

Lost mentors can usually be found. If you lose touch, take the time to reconnect. A meaningful voice or message from the past can be a powerful boost for both mentor and mentee. Regardless of the time lost, the reunion will likely create yet another influence.

6. Convey your story.

You don't have to write a book to communicate to your mentor the importance of the very specific experiences you had with them that shaped your life choices. You can find easier ways. You may be surprised to find out that they never knew you considered them important.

5. Share your accomplishments.

One of the best ways to show gratitude to your mentor is to share your success. We all share pride in the success of those we think we influenced, whether we are responsible for the specific accomplishments or not.

4. Return the favor.

Find ways to give back to mentors who have had an impact. As mentors age, or simply need help, mentees should find ways to return the favor. Mentors "pay forward" with their investments. They will enjoy an occasional return on that investment.

3. Mentor the next generation.

If you are a father, make certain you understand the primary role you play as a mentor. Whether or not you have your own children, find a way to mentor other young people. Volunteer with a formal organization, or simply make time for relatives and friends who need the support of an adult.

2. Help others mentor.

We need an army of highly engaged mentors to guide the next generation. There are many ways to build this army. Spend time helping a new father. Find and support a formal fathering or mentoring organization. Share your time, talent, and treasure in assuring that all children build rich memories of time with their mentors.

1. Live the lessons learned.

The most direct and meaningful way to honor your mentors is to live a life that reflects their influence.

Get Involved in Shaping the Next Generation

As a father, a mentor, or an active participant, you can shape the next generation through involvement in any number of youth development activities and organizations. Nearly every community has a wide variety of resources to support fathers in their important role, and to encourage others to be engaged as caring role models.

These local resources are found in friends and neighbors, faith organizations, schools, athletic teams, and other youth development efforts. Ask around at your schools, religious organizations, and libraries. You'll find many ways to help young people. Get involved and stay involved!

In addition to local resources, the following national organizations provide highly reputable resources and support for fathers, potential mentors, and others interested in promoting the well-being of our next generation.

FATHER RESOURCES

National Center for Fathering
www.fathers.com

National Fatherhood Initiative
www.fatherhood.org/fathers

MENTOR RESOURCES

National Mentoring Partnership
www.mentors.org

The National Mentoring Alliance
www.youthbuild.org/national-mentoring-alliance

Big Brother Big Sister
www.bbbs.org

YOUTH DEVELOPMENT RESOURCES

Institute for Youth Development
www.youthdevelopment.org

4-H Youth Development
www.4-h.org

YMCA
www.ymca.net

Boy Scouts of America
www.scouting.org

Girl Scouts, Inc.
www.girlscouts.org

Acknowledgements

I have the great good fortune of being surrounded by extraordinary people. These people—my friends and family—are my most precious gifts. Our time together shapes my life and contributed substantially to this story.

Ironically, a book about men was made possible by the very special women in my life. My wife, Marti, provided unwavering support and encouragement. As my loving partner in life, she's my trusted sounding board and keeps me grounded.

I also want to thank my mother, Jackie. She's one of the first people I told about writing a work of fiction, and was thrilled that she wouldn't have to read another academic journal article, because, as she put it, "finally something interesting." Maternal bonds run deep, and there's no mistaking the monumental influence she's had on my life. I'd write a book about moms, but I could never adequately capture the depth of their love and commitment.

My two daughters, Amy and Ashley, also motivated me and influenced this effort. I was inspired to tell a story that they, and future generations, would find meaningful. I'm so proud of their early accomplishments in life, and thank them for the joy of watching them grow into caring adults who are changing the world.

The characters in this book are fictional composites of meaningful adults who molded my life. My most influential family, friends, teachers, coaches, and mentors are all represented. I was fortunate to have incredibly strong role models and am confident that those who know them in real life will find their likenesses in these characters.

My good friend and tennis buddy, Bruce Bortz, talked me into publishing this story and took it on as a project. I'm forever thankful for Bruce's sound guidance and personal investment.

This story was written for my father, Ken. It was my gift to him, thanking him for his lifelong gifts to me. I started writing the story to acknowledge his extraordinary influence on my life. I ended by concluding that the book wasn't necessary, at least for him. We acknowledge our mentors best through the choices we make, and can only hope that our gratitude is recognized in how we live.

David Andrews has spent his entire career studying the impact of adults on the emerging lives of children.

As a professor at three major research universities (Oregon State University, Ohio State University, and Johns Hopkins University), he has taught thousands of undergraduate and graduate students while writing extensively about the role of adults in parenting and educating children.

He's a highly regarded national speaker and advocate for children and has been recognized with numerous awards, including distinguished faculty awards from both Oregon State University and Ohio State University, "2003 Distinguished Alumni in Human Sciences" from Florida State University, where he earned his Ph.D., the "2011 Alumnus of the Year" from the Florida Colleges Association, the "2008 Champion of Children for Columbus, Ohio," the "National Family Advocate Award" from the Godman Guild, the "National Friend of Industry Award" from the Education Industry Association, and many others.

Dave earned his A.A. from Pensacola Junior College, his B.A. from Auburn University, and his M.S. from Kansas State University.

He currently resides in Baltimore, MD, where he is Professor and Dean of the School of Education at Johns Hopkins University.

He and his wife have two lovely adult daughters, and thoroughly enjoy their horses and dog.

He wrote *My Father's Day Gift* in honor of his father. It is his first work of fiction.